Nice

&

Naughty

JAYNE RYLON

eBook ISBN: 978-1-941785-22-5
Print ISBN: 978-1-941785-52-2

Cover Art By Jayne Rylon
Interior Print Book Design By Jayne Rylon

Sign Up For The Naughty News!
Contests, sneak peeks, appearance info, and more.
www.jaynerylon.com/newsletter

Shop
Autographed books, reading-themed apparel,
notebooks, totes, and more.
www.jaynerylon.com/shop

Contact Jayne
Email: contact@jaynerylon.com
Website: www.jaynerylon.com
Facebook: Facebook.com/JayneRylon
Twitter: @JayneRylon

OTHER BOOKS BY JAYNE RYLON

DIVEMASTERS
Going Down
Going Deep
Going Hard

MEN IN BLUE
Night is Darkest
Razor's Edge
Mistress's Master
Spread Your Wings
Wounded Hearts
Bound For You

POWERTOOLS
Kate's Crew
Morgan's Surprise
Kayla's Gift
Devon's Pair
Nailed to the Wall
Hammer it Home

HOTRODS
King Cobra
Mustang Sally
Super Nova
Rebel on the Run
Swinger Style
Barracuda's Heart

Touch of Amber
Long Time Coming

COMPASS BROTHERS
Northern Exposure
Southern Comfort
Eastern Ambitions
Western Ties

COMPASS GIRLS
Winter's Thaw
Hope Springs
Summer Fling
Falling Softly

PLAY DOCTOR
Dream Machine
Healing Touch

STANDALONES
4-Ever Theirs
Nice & Naughty
Where There's Smoke
Report For Booty

RACING FOR LOVE
Driven
Shifting Gears

RED LIGHT
Through My Window
Star

Can't Buy Love
Free For All

PARANORMALS
Picture Perfect
Reborn

PICK YOUR PLEASURES
Pick Your Pleasure
Pick Your Pleasure 2

DEDICATION

To AMA

Thank you for your suggestions, both for this story and that I should write at all.

"Keep true to the dreams of thy youth." ~ Friedrich von Schiller

P.S. The answer to my Picture Perfect dedication: 7 days. I stand corrected even though it did take you a year to mention it

CHAPTER ONE

Alexa shifted her convertible into fourth gear with the steady confidence of a seasoned racer. Wind gusts turned shocks of her hair into stinging whips. Her eyes squinted against the sunrays streaming down, guaranteeing sunburn that would peel half her face off. The noise was deafening.

She loved it.

Flying around serpentine curves in the rural landscape, she drank in the fresh mountain air and the beat of the heavy-metal rock screaming from her stereo. Warm, supple leather seats cradled her skin beneath the denim cutoff shorts and halter top she wore.

A refreshing ride provided the escape she needed to blow off some steam after a crazy week wrapping up a consulting project that had consumed her personal time for months. Before shifting lanes to hug the inside edge of the next turn in the deserted road, she glanced in her rearview mirror. A reflected point of light dazzled behind her.

Another vehicle.

Please, don't be a cop.

Alexa slowed to a modest ten miles an hour over the speed limit while debating the likelihood of talking her way out of yet another ticket. This time properly using her turn signal, she merged into the right lane.

When she checked again, the flicker had turned into a full-on blaze. But the machine rapidly gaining on her was no police car. Instead, the silhouette of a man on a motorcycle came into focus. The distance between them shrank steadily as the man partook of a little joy riding of his own.

Mmm mmm.

This was no plastic crotch rocket. A beefy, chrome-and-leather Harley with matching rider closed the gap between them when he accelerated. His black helmet with mirrored visor blocked her view of his face, which beat seeing him clearly. It left her imagination free rein to fill in the blanks, painting him rugged and handsome.

I bet he'll play with me.

She waited until he pulled alongside her sleek, silver graphite car with momentum to pass before she revved the engine. The visor swiveled in her direction, catching her in its reflective surface. Her windblown hair, the glow on her face from the thrill of the ride and her broad smile shone through despite the distortion.

Alexa might have imagined the searing heat of his perusing gaze, but she didn't think so. Raising her eyebrows, she mouthed, "Race?"

His leather-gloved hand came off the handlebar and formed a thumbs up. Damp heat that had nothing to do with the scorching summer day spread between her thighs in anticipation.

Verifying no one else approached behind them, she slowed her car to a stop in the middle of the road. The mystery rider followed suit. He dragged his arm through the air, depicting the likeness of a bridge about a mile down the road.

She nodded in understanding.

A thrill borne from their impending competition raced through her as they both prepared for the launch while the heavy beat of music pumped her up, a perfect background for driving.

This is crazy. What am I doing? Her practical side struggled to surface. Another car could happen along any second, though honestly, the road didn't get much traffic being out in the middle of the national forest. And, hell, hadn't she gone out today looking for some excitement?

She might have backed out if given more time to debate and waffle. The rational facet of her personality dominated most often but at that moment the opportunity for thinking ended. One black-booted foot on the ground, Harley held up three fingers above his palm braced on the broad handlebar. Her calves tensed, poised to let out the clutch and step on the gas as his ring finger folded down leaving two, one...

They both took off, burning rubber that stained the highway behind them.

Alexa timed her start perfectly. Unconcerned, she paced herself as her opponent edged out in front. He easily had her off the line. Nothing she could do about that. The dark rider probably thought the raw power of his bike guaranteed an easy win. But he wouldn't suspect the modifications she'd made to her car. When she pushed the gas pedal to the floor, the high-pitched whine of a turbocharger spooling up overpowered the roar of the engine. When the extra horsepower kicked in, she shot forward, making progress toward catching the man on the bike.

Some part of her mind registered the broad expanse of his back and the way his leather chaps highlighted his jean-clad ass like a gilded frame around a priceless work of art. The ease with which he balanced astride his iron pony seamlessly merged machine and man.

It was like dangling a steak in front of the hounds at the dog track.

She tightened her grip on the gear stick. They weaved down the side of the mountain. Precise maneuvering as she attacked each bend in the road made up for the extra power of his motorcycle. Back and forth. They traded places as the light filtered between the trees in blinding flashes that marked the passing distance.

Off to the left, glimpses of the bridge came into view between the pines. It was going to be close.

One final switchback turn separated them from the finish. She assured herself she'd done this many times before. In fact, she generally drove this way just to see how fast she could make it, each time pushing the limits a little further. Exhilaration blossomed in the pit of her stomach. She'd never dared to try this speed. She had the advantage, though. The optimal line for making the turn originated from her inside lane.

Side by side, they entered the winding section of asphalt. When the biker hesitated, for a fraction of an instant, she gunned it. Tires squealed but held as she zoomed over the wooden structure, overtaking the sexy rider at the finish.

Pumping one fist in the air, Alexa coasted to the shoulder of the road.

A section of the grassy area past the bridge had worn down over time to create a patch of hard-packed dirt people utilized as a parking area when they stopped to admire the view. The rustic arch spanned a sparkling river that cut a swath through the verdant forest surrounding it. Not steep enough to prevent people from walking down safely from above, the hillside tumbled down to form a gorge, which trapped the cooler air coming off the water. It made an ideal spot for swimming, fishing or savoring the peace and solitude of the secluded area.

She burst from her car, still cheering. Mindful not to slam the door, she made her way toward the man on the motorcycle even as he swung his leg over his bike. The elation over victory was heady, making her bolder than usual. She appraised his long limbed frame with blatant curiosity.

Holy hot guy, Batman.

A wave of desire struck her. The aftereffects of her adrenaline rush spiked, demanding an outlet. She absorbed every detail of the fine male specimen standing legs apart in front of her. His impressive build dwarfed her average height, making him well over six feet tall. In addition to his black leather boots, chaps and gloves, his trim hips and athletic form sent a clear message. This was not a man to be messed with. His broad shoulders and bulging arms filled out a scuffed leather jacket creased from molding to his muscles as he rode.

No man had ever looked so good. She wished he would leave his helmet on, allowing her to preserve her mental picture of his matching good looks. That wasn't going to happen, though. He'd already reached up to tug it off.

Breath stuck in her throat as the lower edge of the helmet revealed his gorgeous face inch by inch, like a curtain going up on an ornate stage. Time slowed. In detail unmatched by her wildest fantasies, he showed first the tan skin on his corded neck followed by a strong jaw covered in scruffy stubble the color of expensive cognac. His full, sensual lips showcased his amazing smile. By the time she saw his defined cheekbones and classic nose, she had a serious case of lust. His deep emerald eyes and sandy hair polished off the package.

Her fate was sealed.

Air whooshed from her lungs as the Earth began to rotate again. The intense reaction of her body caused her confident stride to falter. Luckily, he didn't seem to notice. As he hung his helmet on the handlebars with false nonchalance, Mr. Motorcycle kept himself too busy conducting a similar inspection of her physical features to detect the disruption he caused to her system. Alexa felt a little smug, instead of insulted, when his gaze lingered on her curves. She was in deep shit.

"Nice race." He broke the silence before it became awkward. The smoky timbre of his voice curled around her insides, making her shiver despite the heat.

"Not so bad yourself." If genuine arousal didn't course through her, the obvious implication might have embarrassed her. But, somehow, this man triggered a primal reaction. This kind of instant attraction had never happened to her before. It was potent.

You need to get out more.

For such a tall and muscular man, he moved with fluid agility. He peeled off his gloves and tucked them in his back pocket. The gesture caused his black T-shirt, visible between the folds of his now unzipped jacket, to stretch tight over defined pecs. His boots settled directly in front of her thin-soled racing sneakers as he extended his hand.

"Congratulations."

Warmth spread from the intersection of their flesh when she wrapped her fingers around his substantial hand. The brief contact ratcheted up the hormones already raging inside her. After a firm but reasonable squeeze, his fingertips caressed the back of her hand for a moment before they slipped away. Face to face with him, his size, strength and stranger status might have intimidated her on an average day, when she lived in a world of rational thought and practicality. Instead, in this moment, her thoughts centered on what it would be like to be surrounded by all that strapping muscle.

"Thank you." The response meant more than a courtesy. She only indulged her wild streak on rare occasions and he had provided the perfect opportunity with their impromptu race. Although her voice sounded breathy to her own ears, relief flowed over her when he remained unaware of her body's haywire reaction.

His firm bicep brushed the side of Alexa's breast as he continued past her to inspect her car.

Was that an accident? Her nipple didn't care either way. It responded instantly by hardening against the silky fabric of her halter top. Wild and crazy this morning, she'd decided against wearing a bra though she'd never left the house without one before. It was turning into a day of firsts.

She stole the opportunity to verify the view from behind lived up to her memory based on the brief glimpse she'd caught during the race. It did. The man had a killer ass. When he threw a glance, and a devilish smirk, over his shoulder, she guessed he wasn't as oblivious as he seemed.

Their eyes met and she saw an answering spark in his.

"She's beautiful," he murmured reverently.

The car. He's talking about your car. She tried to convince herself, but the rationalization rang false. While he admired the convertible, something more arced between them. Attempting to shake off the unusual reaction inflaming her senses by focusing on her vehicle, Alexa stepped a little closer.

"I've done a lot of work on it."

"Can I touch her?" His implicit understanding of her dislike for people handling her vehicle made her confident he would treat it with the respect it deserved.

"Sure, go ahead." Plus, she got to watch the way his broad finger stroked the defined contour in the flawlessly waxed side panel, which inflamed her senses nearly as much as if he'd placed the caress on her skin instead.

Before she could stop to analyze what her subconscious offered, she asked, "Would you like to take a look under the hood?"

"Hell, yeah."

She had to laugh at the look on his face. "You look like a kid on Christmas."

"It's not every day I come across an opportunity like this." The dark undercurrent of the statement and his piercing green stare made it clear he referred to more than a fancy sports car.

Oh God. He feels it, too.

Alexa should have been freaked out. Alone with a stranger, on a deserted stretch of highway, in the mountains far from the city, sounded like an unwise situation to put herself in. She should be nervous but a remarkable calm surrounded her instead. In fact, she just now realized she'd stopped on the side of the road without a second thought to safety. Today, she threw caution to the wind. The chemical reaction between them affected her like a drug.

As though he sensed her train of thought, the man backed away a few steps, displaying his non-threatening intent. He left the path clear for her to get in her car and drive away but her instincts shouted that she could trust him. She wanted to explore this attraction just a little bit further.

She leaned over the door and rested her fingertips on the hood release. The man's gaze tracked her movement yet he didn't encroach on her space. For a moment, the only sounds breaking the silence were the babble of the stream below, the gentle rustle of leaves from the tree branches overhead and a soft birdsong.

The air between them crackled with tension.

Then, the metallic click of the hood's latching mechanism disengaging relayed her decision to stay. A broad smile spread across his face, raising faint dimples that heightened his attractiveness. Alexa inclined her head in a "come here" gesture as she circled around to the front of the car.

He ambled to her side with a steady gait that made her cognizant of his confidence she wouldn't run. Reaching for the edge of the hood simultaneously, their hands met. Sparks shot up her spine and she jerked. His arm wrapped around her waist in a protective hold. The solid strength kept her from losing her physical footing, but not her emotional balance. This close she could smell the unique combination of his leather gear and subtle, earthy cologne.

"Easy." His hand smoothed down her side and across the top of her ass as he went back to lifting the hood. The blatant touch imbued her with respect for his natural ability to handle a woman. However, she retained enough rationality to admire the gleaming chrome of the engine that she cleaned with painstaking diligence each weekend she could manage the time. Together they leaned forward, caught by the lure of a ridiculously overpowered motor.

"This is an aftermarket addition. Did you do this yourself?" His raised eyebrow conveyed his surprise.

"Yeah."

"I'm impressed. Are you a mechanic?"

"Nope, this is just a hobby." She smirked.

"Some hobby. I *am* a mechanic. This is a damn fine job."

Alexa basked in his appreciation for details. None of her friends understood her devotion to this machine. They couldn't comprehend why she spent the majority of her precious free time refining each tiny part until it was flawless. This man obviously did.

He ran his hand along the connections, searching with deft flicks of his fingertips for imperfections where none existed. His satisfied nod had her beaming.

"Jesus, woman. If someone told me I'd have the chance to play with a car like this today, I'd have said that nothing could distract me. But the way you're looking at me..."

His voice trailed off as she reached up to do a little exploring of her own. Her hand moved on autopilot, following her desire, cupping the side of his stubbled face.

Is this guy for real?

The wet heat of his lips on her palm rasped against her nerves, stronger than any dream. She whimpered as he turned his head to lick the center of her palm before catching the sensitive skin between her thumb and index finger in his teeth in a gentle nip. The move set her ablaze, destroying common sense.

"Kiss me," she demanded.

He didn't need to be told twice. With a low groan, he closed the narrow gap between them, sealing his mouth over hers. He dropped the hood in place and put his hand to better use, wrapping it around her hip, yanking her tight against the hard plane of his chest. His height made Alexa strain on tiptoes to return his kiss. Eager to help, he tucked his other hand around her thigh, just beneath the curve of her ass, and hoisted her up higher on his body.

Even as he bit at her lips, the growing evidence of his desire prodded the fly of her shorts. The denim she wore couldn't prevent the thick ridge of his dick from imprinting the soft curve of her belly as it filled with each rapid beat of his heart, pressing into her. She squirmed against him, instinctively aligning them so her pussy rubbed against the bulge in his jeans.

They fit perfectly together.

Her hands tangled in his hair, loving the way the silky strands teased the sensitive crevices between her fingers. She kneaded his scalp, urging him to take her mouth deeper. His head angled over hers, intensifying the kiss as his tongue lashed playfully against the seam of her lips. She drew it inside her mouth and sucked. He tasted like peppermint.

She moaned with regret when he pulled away.

"I'm going to set you on the hood." He rumbled in her ear in between nibbles of her neck.

"No! Wait."

Though he looked disappointed, he stopped without hesitation.

The heat suffusing her face highlighted her discomfort with being so brazen. "I...I don't want to scratch the paint. Take my shorts off first."

Strained laughter burst from his chest. It transformed his features from rugged to unbearably handsome.

"Honey, you're my every fantasy."

Kneeling in front of her, he flipped up the hem of her shirt to place hungry kisses on her stomach as he unbuttoned her cutoffs. He lowered them down her legs, following the fabric with his mouth, kissing a trail of fire down her inner thighs.

Alexa shuddered when work-roughened hands grabbed her ass and placed her on the car like some erotic hood ornament. Guiding her feet, he rested them on the front fender, straddling his torso. Her arms fell back, braced behind her. Although the metal warmed her skin, bare now except for the sexy thong she wore, the shade kept it from burning her.

His hands ran up her abdomen, pushing the halter top higher to expose her breasts. She would have begged him to touch her but he seemed to know exactly where and how she wanted to be stroked. One of his hands cupped a breast while his tongue laved the aching center of the other. With the side of his face tucked against her skin, which glistened with a fine sheen of perspiration, he looked up.

The desire burning in his eyes matched the lust roaring inside her. Their gazes locked. He waited for her to take the next step.

"More," was all she could say.

"Yes." His hands raked down her torso, fingers grazing each rib with tantalizing precision. When they feathered over her abdomen, her muscles reflexively tightened. Alexa wasn't sure who moaned when the contraction caused the arousal building inside her to flow out onto her pussy lips, soaking the tiny cotton band tucked between her legs.

She thought she heard a gruff, muffled curse just before he tugged the strip of her underwear to the side and buried his face between her legs. Then she didn't care. The combination of her copious fluids and the heat of his mouth against her shaved mound wiped away everything else. When his tongue dipped between her labia to circle her clit she almost came on the spot. His enthusiastic lapping drew out her arousal, which he devoured as though he couldn't get enough of her taste.

Pleasure flowed from his skilled mouth directly into her veins. With her head tilted back, her half-closed eyes facing the fluffy clouds in the perfect blue sky, she concentrated on the intoxicating way he manipulated her flesh and didn't notice his hand moving until the blunt tip of his finger tested her dripping pussy.

She moaned and thrust her hips at his seeking hand. He worked her open, dipping in further each time he drove the digit inside. When his finger tunneled within her, palm facing upwards, he curled the long length until it pressed against her G-spot. The sensation overwhelmed her with pleasure. This man had moves she had only read about.

Hovering on the edge of an orgasm, she shrieked. Mistaking the cry of pleasure for surprise or pain, he paused, keeping her climax just out of reach. In that moment of clarity, she craved more. Having the most amazing orgasm of her life no longer seemed like enough.

"I want you inside me. Now."

It may not have been the most graceful move she ever saw, but he somehow managed to balance her thighs on his shoulders while he ripped his wallet from his back pocket. He retrieved a condom before dropping the billfold on the ground, unconcerned about the rest of the contents. With one hand, he got the button of his jeans undone and the fly spread open. The other hand shoved his pants and dark gray briefs out of the way, allowing him to thread the most magnificent cock she'd ever seen through the opening of his leather chaps.

As he rolled the condom over his raging hard-on, he stepped between her legs and claimed her mouth. This kiss was a thousand times more potent than the first, so stimulating it shocked her. Unrestrained now, he possessed her with a natural dominance that coerced her body to bow even closer to his. While he claimed her mouth, he massaged her clit. The contrast of his harsh kiss and tender teasing had her writhing beneath him.

"Now. Please, now."

His knees bent forward, resting on the edge of the hood, and the head of his cock notched against her a moment before he thrust, driving his broad shaft a few inches inside her tight, clinging sheath. Her arms came up, banding around his solid back.

"You feel so fucking good." He groaned. "I'm not going to last."

The pure passion inflecting his words, combined with the forbidden intensity of the moment, poised her on the edge of climax. He withdrew until only the bulbous head of his cock remained before thrusting. His long, thick cock exhilarated each sensitive nerve ending along the way until her pussy completely encased him. When he tucked his pubic bone against her clit and ground his hips in a provocative circle, she shattered.

His hands clamped around her shoulders, anchoring himself deep inside her. His teeth raked the side of her neck as the waves of orgasm crashed over her again and again. The guttural cry that echoed in the empty ravine as he joined her mirrored her own sense of relief and utter completion.

A startled bird left the tree overhead with a flutter. Then the only sounds filling the void were their harsh breathing, the rustle of leaves in the gentle breeze and the tick of the engine cooling beneath her ass.

Limp, Alexa lay draped across the hood of the car, her legs splayed on either side of his tapered waist as she struggled to catch the breath he'd stolen from her. Slowly, very slowly, the world sharpened into focus. He shifted above her, slipping out of the swollen channel of her sex. She sighed at the loss.

He braced himself on his elbows and looked down into her eyes with a soulful gaze before speaking.

"My name is Justin."

And just like that, the spell broke.

She flinched and rolled from the hood, forcing him to step back to keep his balance.

He must have read the horror on her face because he started scrambling to adjust his clothes.

"Shit, don't do that. Don't go." Instead of halting her, the frustrated order spurred her on.

She grabbed her shorts from the ground and stepped into them with the practice of someone who often gets called out of the house on emergencies during the night. She was already in the driver's seat, starting the car, by the time he had gathered his wallet, its scattered contents, and regrouped enough to start after her.

"Damn it, tell me your name!"

Alexa shook her head in denial before throwing the car in gear and peeling out of the parking area without a thought for the damage rocks or sticks kicked up against the paint could do. She fought tears when she looked in her rearview mirror and saw him kick the trunk of the tree they'd made love under.

No, fucked under. She'd gone temporarily insane and had sex with a perfect stranger whose name she hadn't even known.

What the hell came over me?

CHAPTER TWO

"It was bound to happen sooner or later." Jamie sat across the high top table from Alexa and tried to alleviate some of the misery bubbling inside her best friend. "Sweetie, you were like a sexual pressure cooker. Something had to give."

"Jamie, were you listening? I had sex with a total stranger. In broad daylight. Where anyone might have seen us. I must be insane!" Alexa dropped her head between her hands. Her professional façade never cracked like this at work. Even now, most people wouldn't see the distress harbored within the polished businesswoman perched on the stool next to Jamie in their office building's coffee shop. But she had taken one look at Alexa's normally meticulous appearance this morning and noticed her mismatched earrings. Then, when the other woman almost forgot her eight o'clock meeting, it confirmed Jamie's suspicions. Something serious had upset her friend, she never missed an appointment. Maybe...

"Were you careful?"

Alexa grimaced. "No, I just told you..."

"I mean, did you use protection?" If she didn't look so wretched, Jamie might have laughed.

"Oh. Uh, yeah, he did." Her friend turned a delicate shade of red, her fingernails tapping on the paper wrapper around her drink. "But, honestly, if he hadn't thought of it, I probably wouldn't even have noticed."

"Then it was good?" Jamie grinned, delighted someone had blasted through the calm reserve Alexa wrapped around her like a shield.

"God, I've never felt anything like it before," she admitted. Her eyes glazed in reverie for a moment before she stammered. "But that's not the point. Jamie, I can't believe I did something so stupid, so fucking irresponsible."

"Well I, for one, am glad you did. I keep telling you these men you date can't give you what you need. You're never satisfied with them." Jamie sighed. Sometimes a friend just had to tell it like it was. "Girl, I wouldn't even call most of them dates. The suits attend professional functions with you. They have different names, sure, but they're all stamped from the same mold. Boring, boring, boring."

Jamie knew she might be getting somewhere when Alexa didn't even try to refute it. "They may be boring, but they're dependable, conservative and respectable. Wild guys aren't good relationship material."

"How would you know, Alexa? Just 'cause one jerk burned you doesn't mean men who are adventurous and trustworthy don't exist."

"I don't believe it. Those traits are mutually exclusive. And that's the problem. I want both. No, I *need* both but it's not worth wishing for the impossible." Jamie could practically see her friend rebuilding herself, reassembling the fractured pieces of her emotions as she fortified her resolve by chugging the last of her hazelnut coffee. "And right now, I have to get upstairs and start researching the Winston project proposal."

The discussion effectively closed, Alexa hopped off the stool onto her sleek, four-inch heels.

Jamie smiled. Alexa would recover. Too bad. She could have used an insatiable, daring man to help her relieve the tension from her stressful job. "Well, you know I'm always here if you need to talk. Or decide to give me the juicy details."

Alexa closed the distance between them and embraced her in a brief but tight hug. "Thanks, Jamie."

***

Alexa tucked the tall leather chair under the polished surface of the substantial boardroom table and began unpacking her briefcase. She represented Therber Management Services at today's proposal. If she won this contract, as a merger and acquisition consultant for Winston Industries, her burgeoning career would be assured.

Instead of rehearsing her strategy, as she normally would while organizing her documents in precise rows before her, she surveyed the scenery out the twenty-third-story window. In addition to the traffic rushing below her in a blur of lights, and the faint sounds of the city drifting up in a cacophony of horns and squeaky breaks, she glimpsed the rolling hills on the horizon. Larger steel and glass buildings, like this one housing Winston's corporate headquarters, surrounded her own office and blocked the distracting view. Otherwise, she might never get any work done.

Her gaze landed on the distant landscape, causing memories of the race to flare in her mind. No matter how stupid it had been, that stolen afternoon's passion still had the power to set her body on fire weeks later. The grueling hours spent on this proposal had kept her from dwelling on the incident overmuch. Add mental distraction to the list of reasons this contract was essential. If she won it today, her work would have just begun. Otherwise, she'd have lots of time on her hands to brood when she got fired for losing such an important opportunity.

She tore her focus from the lulling purple hue of the distant mountains and wondered if she should switch places to face away from the distraction. J. Winston, CEO of Winston Industries, possessed a reputation as a fierce negotiator and competitor. She required complete concentration to deal with the eccentric entrepreneur. He hired only the best on a regular basis and this deal was anything but ordinary. The top secret project required intense business acumen, speed to market and a reliable partner.

The venture had the business community talking. J. Winston always inspired gossip due to his reclusive nature. Some called him The Wizard because no one but his innermost circle ever saw him, and no picture of him existed that she could find in her extensive research. He stayed in his tower, pulling levers, deciding the fates of companies from a distance.

If you believed the buzz, he'd reached out for a consultant because he didn't trust even his top staff with the sensitivity of this latest project. He needed someone new, fresh and unbiased. Someone a competitor couldn't have persuaded to go mole. The full extent of the assignment remained hidden from the management firms bidding for the contract but that didn't squash Alexa's confidence that she could facilitate whatever scheme Winston Industries, and their mysterious leader, cooked up.

The heavy solid wood door swung open admitting an intimate group of executives she recognized on sight, either through the numerous networking events she attended as part of her routine duties or due to her background investigation on Winston Industries.

Game time. She stood, greeting each one by name, utterly calm and collected. The rush brought on by intense situations filled her now, just as it did when she went out driving. When everyone claimed a seat, only one chair—opposite the broad table from her—remained unoccupied. She flicked a subtle glance at her watch with thirty seconds to the scheduled meeting time.

Alexa flipped through her mental notes on the interests of those present, constructing calculated filler to entertain the staff and start selling herself to them in the ten minutes or so that it would take for J. Winston to arrive fashionably delayed. Many executive officers channeled a more powerful image by making their appointments wait. Therefore, he surprised and impressed her with his punctuality when he appeared through a private entrance just a few moments later, precisely on time.

She recovered from that slight miscalculation with tact, but nothing could have prepared her for the man that strode past the wall of windows, stopping right in front of her, hand outstretched. Automatically, she took it, wondering at the difference in his firm grip now that he tendered it in a professional gesture rather than the fiery grasp of their tryst. She squeezed his fingers, trying desperately not to think of the time they'd spent exploring deep inside her.

Holy shit.

At least she knew what the J. in J. Winston stood for now.

Justin.

Their grip extended longer than etiquette required, or found polite, but she couldn't seem to disengage from the desire that bloomed inside her at even this miniscule touch. She studied his face, instantly recognizable and somehow different from the day they'd met out on the road. His smooth jaw, shaved clean of the scruffy stubble, complimented the impeccable hairstyle that probably cost more than she made in a month. The charcoal suit he wore packaged the sexy body underneath like an exquisitely wrapped gift, making her want to rip off the covering to find the goodies hidden beneath it. His gleaming smile seemed genuine, and innocent.

Justin's professional reaction doused her initial fear that he would recoil upon finding her in his boardroom. She could act cool, too.

In the next moment, she expected him to say something like, "So good to see you again." Or "I'm glad to officially be introduced." But, instead, he said, "It's very nice to meet you. I've heard many good things about your work and look forward to hearing your presentation today." Then he crossed to his side of the table and sat down with an expectant nod, cueing her to begin, as though he hadn't just dropped a bomb on her.

To steady her churning thoughts, Alexa turned away under the pretense of tweaking settings on her laptop and the attached projector, although she had taken care of those details long before the meeting started. Several emotions crashed through her system at once. A dose of relief he hadn't called her out mixed with embarrassment.

Does he think I'm a slut? Her uncertainty washed away beneath the force of lust, which spiked off the charts as that amazing chemical reaction spread through her again. Finally, anger joined the swirling mass inside her and stuck. *He doesn't want anyone to know we've met.*

A ball of emotion lodged in her throat but she wouldn't let Justin ruin this chance. Even if he played some cruel game, she wanted the other powerful attendees to maintain their good opinions of her work. Afterward, she would deal with him in private.

Professionalism rose to the surface, driving her onward, and she buried her doubts.

She collected herself, drew a deep breath and focused on the strategy she had devised as she began to work the room. "Today, I will prove to you that I am the only consultant that measures up to Winston Industries' standards for your upcoming project."

***

J. Winston observed the polished performance of Ms. Alexa Daniels in utter fascination. An underlying aloof chill, which mesmerized and intrigued him, marred her perfect façade. The unexpected, illogical reaction roused his mistrust as well. He couldn't afford surprises on this deal and he had considered her a sure thing.

What is she trying to hide?

He reclined in his chair, linking his fingers together over his abdomen. Though she continued the well-executed presentation, he noticed the dilation of her pupils and the tiniest shake of the red laser pointer's dot on her screen each time she glanced at him. Did desire cause this anomaly in her behavior? He didn't consider it conceited to appraise her attraction to him. If he hired her, they would work closely together. This deal had the potential to boost his company out of reach of their competitors for a hundred years. The revolutionary technology he had discovered would be profitable only if they could harness the competitive advantage first. He wouldn't risk an opportunity like that on something as fleeting as lust, no matter how sizzling.

He had studied Alexa for a long time, tracked her career for years as she rose through the ranks at Therber, gaining the experience she needed to become a valuable asset to his organization. He'd joined today's meeting convinced it would conclude with an offer. Maybe a permanent one.

Now, he considered her behavior and knew that he didn't have all the pieces. He hadn't factored in the obvious magnetism that drew them to each other. Her file photos had always struck him as oddly attractive, though her beauty wasn't conventional. Still, that didn't explain her unusual reaction to him. She impressed him with her ability to mask the turmoil the others didn't notice, only allowing subtle hints through for him to perceive.

She's angry. In addition to the attraction rolling off her, he distinguished the other variety of heat. He prided himself on being able to read people, that skill alone contributed greatly to his success. She wrapped up the briefing having convinced the others on the panel of her worth. He interpreted their sanction in the way they nodded with her every assertion, hungry for more, leaning forward in attention. Everyone turned to him, waiting for his response.

"I'd like to speak with Ms. Daniels privately." Collectively, they rose, filing out of the boardroom, offering their support to her via handshakes and nods of approval when they passed.

Her disposition changed the moment he heard the door thunk closed.

"What the hell is going on?" She leaned forward, her arms locked straight, palms flat on the table as she unleashed the blistering sentiment he'd glimpsed earlier. Her auburn hair bounced in soft curls, framing the deceptive softness of her face, tumbling into the V-neck of that delicate lace camisole beneath her tailored suit jacket. He pried his eyes from the hint of soft, round flesh.

Whoa. Years had passed since a prospective client dared talk to him like that. Her attitude shouldn't have thrilled him and, yet, it did.

Something dark awoke inside him as the hunt began in earnest. Usually, he could tamp down the primal segment of his nature but this woman drew it out of him in spades. Now that she showed her hand, instead of trying to deceive him by shuttering her buried emotions, he knew he wanted her. For his project.

Yeah, and that's not all.

"I believe we just completed your proposal process. This is the part where I offer you the job." He selected his words with care. Her reaction perplexed him but determination ensured he would discover the source of her hostility and eradicate her objections. He would have her.

"Process? So this has been an ongoing interview?" Her voice chilled further.

"Of course. You're too savvy to assume I'd hire you without considerable investigation." He thought of the hours he'd reviewed reports on her over the years. She controlled her flinch but he caught the ghost of the motion anyway.

"I didn't expect you to come off your throne to inspect me so personally. If you think for one minute that I would take a position with you after this, you're crazy. I don't care how powerful you are or how important this deal is. Count me out." Alexa gathered her briefcase, abandoning the presentation materials where they lay, broadcasting her intention to walk out if he didn't stop her.

"Wait." He rose, blocking her path. The warm scent of spring wafted up to him.

One of the reasons he kept out of the limelight was to avoid the women who came on to him for his money or for advancement. Under usual circumstances, attraction sent up a red flag, a warning to avoid a female business partner but, for once, he felt compelled to investigate. Electric sparks of desire lured him closer to this woman when he should have dusted his hands.

She stopped practically on top of him as she tried to squeeze past. Her chest pressed close to his upper abdomen, more petite than the shadow her iron demeanor cast. When their eyes met they both hesitated, stunning him with the force of his reaction to her.

"Don't go." He couldn't prevent the command from sounding so harsh.

"I didn't listen the last time you ordered me to stay, why do you think it'll work now?" Her bitterness sliced through the haze infiltrating his mind.

"We've met before?"

"Yeah, when I was crazy enough to let you fuck me. Or do you nail women on the hoods of their cars so often that you actually forgot?" Disgust permeated her voice and her features. It cut him to know that she aimed some of the hostility at herself.

Oh, God, it can't be her. Some glimmer of realization must have crossed his face because she snapped off their eye contact and bustled past him to the door. Just before it closed completely she spun around. Hurt mixed with the heat that, even now, lingered in her gorgeous brown eyes.

"Go to hell, Justin."

He stared at the spot she had stood only a moment ago as reality sank in. His mind formulated a plan while he made his way into his personal office. From there he followed her descent down the elevator and exit from the building on the security cameras even as he hit the first speed dial number programmed in his cell.

Ringing came over the line as she stormed out to the parking garage.

Come on, answer!

"Yo." His brother's characteristic, informal greeting came at the same moment Alexa reached her car.

"Son of a bitch!" On the screen, she tucked her slender frame into a hot little convertible.

"What's up, Jay?" The voice picked up some uneasiness.

"Justin, I found your woman."

CHAPTER THREE

"**W**hat? Who is she?" Justin's inflection became alert, the lazy cadence exchanged for rapt attention. "Where is she?"

"We have a problem." His seriousness dissolved the initial thrill in his brother's intonation. Even over the phone their communication extended beyond words. They understood each other in ways other people could never fathom.

"Fuck. Why does everything have to be complicated?"

Jason laughed despite the situation. For twins, identical in so many ways, they possessed polar opposite personalities. Where he required structure, Justin enjoyed being carefree and uninhibited. It was one of the reasons they made a perfect team. Together, they would sort this out.

"Can you meet me at 534 Lennox Road in thirty minutes?" Jason read off the address from Alexa's file lying open on his desk. He multitasked, clicking through his calendar, clearing all his other appointments for the afternoon. This woman held the key for them both.

"I'll make it in twenty." Justin loved speed and, on top of that, he'd spent weeks obsessed with finding this woman.

Jason looked at the phone. The severed connection didn't stop him from admonishing his brother. "Be careful."

***

Alexa fumed as she maneuvered her car through heavy rush hour traffic.

Shit, why do I care if he wants to pretend it never happened?

Mr. Winston, she thought snidely, presented her with a golden opportunity to banish her indiscretion into oblivion and take on a professional challenge of a career-making magnitude. But how could she stand to work for a man capable of such complete deception? Her morals wouldn't allow it. After all, that asshole had pursued her for business purposes and didn't even have the decency to feign guilt for enjoying fucking her on the side of the road under false pretenses. She didn't doubt that he'd enjoyed it, some things a man couldn't fake, but apparently their interlude had been a necessary evil. She wondered if he'd given himself hazard pay for that duty.

You're just pissed he wasn't as affected as you.

Every day of the past two weeks she'd buried herself in work only to find that nothing could douse the yearning he'd ignited. His calculated seduction stung and confused her. What purpose could it serve? Logic suggested insurance, an imprudence to hold over her as blackmail in case she attempted to reveal his trade secret. *Damn, this must be one important deal.*

Not even for that would she risk her heart. As much as it frustrated her, she admitted the truth—that Justin had turned out to be a slimy dirtbag—hadn't obliterated her physical attraction to him. She wouldn't lose her head over another undeserving creep. She made a point of learning from her mistakes so she understood this insane attraction would have her tangled up in emotions before long if she didn't escape while she still had the chance.

God, he looked good in that suit.

"Shit! I am so screwed." Not only did she face getting fired for blowing the proposal, but also she hungered for something she could never have. The rough and wild man she met on that sunlit road never truly existed.

Alexa turned into the underground parking facility attached to her well-maintained condo, surprised to find herself home so soon. Her wandering thoughts had kept her driving on autopilot. A creature of habit, she pulled into her usual spot and dropped her forehead on the leather steering wheel while gathering energy to make the hike through the desolate cement garage in her power heels.

Fat lot of good those did you. She climbed from the low seat, bitching to herself as she discovered her day hadn't hit rock bottom yet. When she reached for her briefcase on the passenger seat, something hard and cold jabbed the ridge of her spine. One clammy hand covered her mouth as a steely arm encircled her chest, jerking out of the car.

"Keep still, be quiet and I won't hurt you."

Like she believed anything a man holding a gun on her promised. She kicked backward and her stiletto gouged his shin. The rasping voice turned shrill and mean as he cursed her.

"Nice try, bitch." This time when he grabbed her, he didn't pretend to be rational. His fingers latched onto her upper arm with bruising force. He slammed her face down on the trunk of her car causing agony to radiate from her ribs, driving the wind from her momentarily.

"I don't have any cash on me." She masked her fear by giving rage free rein.

"It's not your fucking money I want." The coarse sound he made couldn't be called a laugh. "I need to know what he's planning."

"Who?" Genuine confusion colored her reflexive question.

"Don't play dumb, whore. I can make you talk." She fought the urge to retch when the man pinned her with his body, trapping her tight enough to show her how much hurting her excited him. "What is Winston up to?"

"I don't know." She answered honestly, understanding he'd never believe her.

Her assailant shook her with rough jerks, twisting her arm up behind her back. She thrashed in his hold and heard her skirt rip as it caught on a metal edge that sliced her skin beneath it. Alexa couldn't stifle the cry he wrung from her as he applied more pressure.

"Hello?" A deep voice rang out from several rows away, echoing in the cavernous space. "Is someone down here?"

Her captor tried to cover her mouth but, with the gun in one hand and the other holding her arm, he couldn't move fast enough.

"Help!" She screamed so loud the raw sound that tore from her throat hurt her own ears. With her head forced to the side, mashed against the trunk, she glimpsed a mop of sandy hair bobbing as the newcomer ran closer. His sharp footfalls grew louder as the man behind her dragged her toward a beat up old van parked nearby.

"Hey, you!" Her would-be savior bore down on them as he sprinted between the cars. "Get your fucking hands off her."

She struggled, kicking and fighting every inch of the way, but when the sharp corner of the vehicle's sliding door banged against her elbow, she knew time had run out. By mere chance, her thrashing knee connected with something soft as the lunatic attempted to shove her through the opening. She half-fell, half-scurried away as his hold loosened for an instant. His moan of pain and frustration cut off abruptly, silenced by the peel of tires, as his driver carried them away a moment before the helpful stranger reached her.

He skidded across the last few feet, rushing to her side.

"Jesus Christ! Are you okay?" He knelt next to her, his hands searching for injuries. "Where are you hurt?"

"I'm fine." The thready croak didn't inspire much confidence.

"We have to get out of here. If they didn't know where you lived before, they do now."

His familiar voice arrowed through her shock and thawed her stunned mind. "Justin?"

"Yeah, honey, it's me." She hadn't recognized him at first. The polished businessman had morphed into the rugged rebel of her dreams. Alexa flinched when her hand touched the short whiskers she remembered so well. "You're safe. It's okay now."

He seemed to be trying to convince himself. While he cradled her in the crook of one arm, sheltering her, he extracted a sleek cell phone from the inside pocket of his leather jacket. Scrambled thoughts untangled themselves as she wrestled to contain the tremors beginning to shake her.

"You have a beard." Unsteady fingers pressed against scruffy hairs and the tense jaw beneath them.

"Hate to shave." He might have continued their surreal conversation but someone answered his call. "Jay, where the hell are you?"

J. Not Justin.

Oh, shit. J. must think she was insane. She feared she might be sick as her thoughts zigzagged between the attack and her colossal screw up in the boardroom. She barely registered Justin arguing in the background.

"I don't give a fuck if it's reserved for residents. Just get in the damn garage. Someone attacked her." He snapped the phone closed.

"Can you stand up?" He searched the lot, his eyes never resting on one spot for long. His vigilance bolstered her survival instincts, giving her the strength to start moving again. As he helped her gain her feet, a luxurious sedan rolled up beside them. "Just a few more seconds, honey."

He ushered her inside the door he yanked open. Her scraped knees burned as she crawled across the backseat. She met the driver's gaze in the rearview mirror.

"Someone better tell me what's going on here." The shaking of her body affected her voice, making the words jitter. Both men exchanged looks, drawing her attention. They were so alike and, yet, so different. "You're twins."

"Yes." Clean-shaven answered the rhetorical question. "Justin, make sure we're not followed."

"Where are you taking me?" Neither brother answered, their attention on the traffic streaming by.

She declined to object further since throbbing pain began to seep through her adrenaline rush. The first few minutes passed in a tense silence. Both J. and Justin concentrated on the cars surrounding them but Justin never let go of her hand. The warm reassurance his touch instilled bolstered her courage as she recovered from the surprise of the attack. She began to relax into the plush upholstery.

"Jay, we're clear, pick up the pace." Justin sat tense beside her, his foot in constant motion, tapping against the floorboard.

"I know it kills you to let me drive," J. said. Truth be told, J. irked her, too. He drove like a ninety-year-old woman, exactly at the speed limit, a precise four-second gap between his suave-but-safe vehicle and the car in front of them, never violating a single rule. The steady calm J. harnessed clearly escaped his brother. "But anyone watching has to believe there's nothing out of the ordinary if they're looking for Alexa."

"Alexa, nice." Justin tested out her name, causing a shiver to run down her spine at the way he savored the word. Still, she couldn't afford to be distracted.

"We're not going to the police?" They headed in the opposite direction of the station on the freeway.

"No. It's too dangerous. They'll expect us to, and I'm afraid the stakes are too high now." J. met her eyes with a brief stare in the rearview mirror. "I'm sorry for getting you mixed up in this."

The dark-tinted windows sheltered them from unwanted attention, cocooning them in privacy. Convinced they'd reached safety, Justin turned his attention to her. His eyes darkened as he took her in.

She opened her mouth to continue questioning them when he interrupted.

"You're bleeding."

"Shit, I'm sorry. Did I get any on the seat?" Alexa glanced down at the gash in her leg she hadn't noticed while checking for suspicious vehicles. She tugged on the ripped material of her suit skirt, tearing off a dangling section to compress against the cut. A red stain grew across the patch in a few seconds.

"Like I care about that." J. muttered from the front. "Does she need a doctor?"

Justin reached over to add light pressure with one hand while he probed her side. "I saw that bastard slam you against your car. You're going to be bruised, but I don't think anything's broken. Nothing we can't handle ourselves, Jay." Fury turned his words to acid. He lifted his head, meeting her gaze full on for the first time since he rescued her.

The combination of his fingers on her thigh and his palm so near her breast had her gasping for air.

"Does that hurt?" Worry crossed his face, drawing his mouth into a thin line.

She shook her head and scooted away from him. It was impossible to think when he touched her. "I want to know what's going on. Right now."

"You got me." He shrugged. "But I'd sure as hell like to know, too."

CHAPTER FOUR

J.'s audible exhalation reached Alexa. "I knew this was going to turn into a cluster fuck."

"What are you into, Jay?" Justin asked the question she burned to know the answer to.

"First things first." J. couldn't ignore the social niceties. "I'm Jason Winston. Justin, I believe you've met Alexa Daniels before."

She caught the knowing look the twins exchanged but her attention shifted when Justin made a sound somewhere between a moan and a sigh. "Yeah." He turned to her with an honesty she couldn't deny. "I've been looking all over for you. I had no idea you knew my brother."

"I don't." Some of her indignation returned. "Are you saying all of this is coincidence?"

"Considering I don't even know what 'all of this' is? Yeah, that's what I'm saying." Frustration escalated in his words. Every one of his reactions seemed frank and uncensored.

"He didn't know who you were. I swear it." A promise from a man like Jason could be trusted implicitly.

"And you?" Her eyebrow arched.

"I've followed your career for several years," he admitted.

"What!" Betrayal colored Justin's outburst. "You knew I wanted her, I've been going crazy trying to track her down."

"Relax." Though he addressed Justin, Alexa understood he intended his words for both of them. "I didn't realize she was your woman. I never would have matched her profile with your description."

"I'm my own woman." Her face flamed with a mixture of irritation and arousal. She averted her eyes in an attempt to hide the reaction. The four-lane road had given way to a rural street. No pursuers could hide from them here, she could see for miles on the secluded road in either direction. By the looks of the pristine lawns, manicured formal landscaping and winding drives, the neighborhood catered to wealthy residents seeking privacy.

"Amen." Justin's rough reply accompanied a soft laugh from the front seat. The temperature climbed a few degrees inside the cabin of the car.

"We made it." Jason's announcement couldn't have come at a better time. It cut off their discussion. Both men focused on scanning the yard in front of the massive stone wall and iron gate as Jason buzzed it open.

He guided the car into the bay in front of them. They stayed in place until the garage door shut, concealing them from outside, then Justin slid his arms beneath her and plucked her from the car. He carried her into the house through the door Jason held for them, their actions so synchronized they appeared choreographed. The brothers moved, working as one, without talking. Justin acted while Jason took care of the details, flicking on lights, turning off the security alarm and heading upstairs to gather supplies.

The thick muscles of Justin's arms secured her to his chest. She gave in to temptation and snuggled close to him, drinking in his body heat and laying her palm over his collarbone.

"You smell like motor oil," Alexa mumbled against his neck, insanely enticed to lick it.

"Came straight from work."

"I love that smell." She felt, rather than heard, the rumble he made low in his throat.

His fingers tightened on her knee and he brushed her forehead with his lips a moment before he deposited her on the marble top of the kitchen island. The stone shocked her, so cold compared to the toasty security of his body. It snapped her from the sensual trance being too near him lulled her into.

She took in the well-appointed cooking area with its stainless-steel appliances and large eat-in dining area. For a space so richly designed, it managed to maintain a cozy, welcoming atmosphere.

"You both live here?"

Justin nodded as he turned on the faucet in the sink beside her. He grabbed a large ceramic bowl from a cabinet behind them. His shoulders rippled and flexed beneath his form fitting T-shirt as he reached up to the top shelf.

An answering clench echoed through her abdomen, her body responding to his nearness. The need to touch him, to have him close to her again, grew inside. One thing was certain, the wild attraction they'd shared that day on the side of the road hadn't been a one time, freak occurrence. No matter how she'd tried to reason it away while falling asleep over the past two weeks, their affair hadn't been the result of her too long stretch of abstinence, high stress levels or a bout of temporary insanity. He turned her on like no other man.

Except his brother.

She squashed the stray thought before she could examine it further.

Jason strode into the room, first aid kit in one hand and a large fluffy bathrobe draped over a sinewy forearm. Somewhere along the way, he'd gotten rid of the suit jacket, rolled up his shirtsleeves and unbuttoned his collar. He'd maintained his crisp appearance, looking totally unruffled, even after the hectic afternoon. His steady reliability appealed to her as much as Justin's untamed streak.

Justin soaked a clean dishrag in the lukewarm water and placed it on top of the cloth sticking to her oozing cut. "You got it in there?" He didn't even have to look up and make eye contact for his twin to understand his meaning.

"Yeah." The soft light of regret in Jason's eyes made it clear she wasn't going to like whatever they implied.

"Have what?" She asked, lost amid their unspoken conversation.

"Suture supply kit." Justin's blunt answer made her cringe. She turned squeamish at the thought of metal piercing the raw wound on her leg.

"I don't think that's necessary," she tried objecting. Alexa started to shove off the counter but each brother put out a hand in unison to prevent her from hopping down. Jason held one hip while Justin stroked the other.

"You don't want a scar to mess up that sexy thigh." Justin slipped between her legs, his abdomen pressing against her core. One broad finger reached up to tuck her hair behind her ear. The sight of his blackened fingernail, where he'd obviously smashed it, and calloused hand only increased his attractiveness. Her body betrayed her, turning pliant and greedy. Instead of pushing him away, she wrapped her fist in his shirt and tugged him closer.

His smile hovered a millimeter away from touching her. "I missed you," he whispered and licked her with the tip of his tongue, soothing the swollen spot where she'd bitten her lip earlier. She moaned, all thoughts but sinking into his touch vaporized when he kissed her. He cupped her breast as his tongue probed her mouth, stroking her with a sweet, candid fervor. Alexa arched closer, her skirt riding high up on her thighs.

Then something cool and slippery spread across her skin before the initial sting of the needle pricked her leg. *What the hell?*

The passion Justin sparked in her narrowed her world to his touch and the intense pleasure he gave her. She'd forgotten his brother stood less than a foot away on the other side of her leg. She struggled against Justin's hold but he clasped her tighter and continued to seduce her.

"Let him distract you, sweetheart." Jason's metered voice came soft and rational in her ear. His unwavering hand guided the thread. "I'm trained in first aid. I used a topical anesthetic but it's still going to be uncomfortable. I don't want you to hurt any more than you have to."

She whimpered. She had no desire to experience more than the first few passes he'd already made. She surrendered to Justin's touch. His mouth persuaded her to forget everything but him. She sipped at his lips and leaned into his embrace.

"That's it, Alexa." Jason crooned his encouragement. "Good girl."

She spread her thighs wider, allowing Justin room to fit tight to her. The cool air of the kitchen washed over the saturated crotch of her racy panties a moment before the ridge of his hardening cock stirred against her aching pussy. Breaking the taboo of privacy by inviting Jason to watch their carnal interaction unlocked a secret chamber of arousal she hadn't known existed within her. Nervousness fought with the desire attempting to overwhelm her.

"Just relax, baby." Jason soothed both her worry over the physical discomfort and the greater panic threatening her when she realized how much she enjoyed their forbidden display. She hardly felt the deft touch of Jason's hand on her thigh. "Justin will give you an orgasm if you let him."

The combination of Jason's reserved narration and Justin's scalding touch fueled her needs. It was like being trapped between fire and ice. She moaned as Justin rocked against her. One hand supported her back while the other teased her steel hard nipple. Lust built inside her quickly, just as it had two weeks before. She strained against him, helping him stroke her clit just the way she needed it.

"You like that?" She couldn't have answered Jason's question even if she tried. The domineering control in his voice set her nerves on end, coercing her to submit.

Justin took the opportunity to explore her neck, licking and biting, as he became engrossed in the moment, trusting his brother to guide the encounter.

"Yes. Please," she begged. Her head dropped against her shoulder blades as every muscle in her body devoted itself to enhancing the sensations driving her closer to rapture.

"Please what?" It seemed natural to meet Jason's commanding gaze. The banked yearning in his eyes urged her higher. His discipline coupled with the wild abandon of his twin plunged her deeper into the exhilaration of the moment. She had never considered exhibitionism before, but having both men focused on her created a whole new level of pleasure. Her insides fluttered as she spiraled closer to climax. Just a few more seconds of Justin's intimate grind and she would go over the edge.

She kept her eyes on Jason's smoldering look when she said, "I need him to make me come."

Jason's broad smile dripped with hunger, "And I need to see it."

As soon as the words left his brother's mouth, Justin rotated his hips in an irresistible rhythm. Contractions started forming deep in her pussy and her channel clenched desperately.

"Now, Alexa," Jason ordered, his voice clear and in control. "Come for us."

In front of her, Justin roared as she grasped him around the waist with her legs and clung. He tried to wrench away but she rode his erection through their clothes. The orgasm shattered her. Even as her body shook and spasmed, she stared into the deep, still pools of Jason's eyes until Justin's groan of completion took her by surprise.

He recaptured her mouth and thrust against her in short, rapid jerks of his hips that enhanced her never-ending orgasm as he spilled his come. For a moment, all three of them maintained a stunned silence filled only with their harsh breathing in the aftermath of their outburst of passion but Jason broke the tension with a derisive laugh and a slap on his brother's back.

"I swear I haven't come in my jeans in twenty years." Justin's humor tempered his dismay. He rested his forehead against Alexa's and framed her face with his hands. His thumbs rubbed her cheekbones in a tender gesture. "You're amazing."

She avoided the emotion bared in his expression—too much, too soon.

"Will you finish the stitches now, so I can go take a shower?" She regretted the puzzled look her withdrawal caused Justin but Jason nodded in simple understanding.

"It was done a long time ago." He helped her slide out from Justin's loose hold and set her gently on the ground before handing her the fluffy robe he'd set aside earlier. "Go ahead, everything else you need is in the room at the top of the stairs. Make yourself at home."

She turned and walked away, desperate not to limp or glance over her shoulder. One moment of weakness and she'd end up right back in their arms, but she needed time to sort out all that had happened.

The light blue walls and deep, plush carpeting of the guest room soothed her frazzled nerves. She undressed gingerly, careful of the aches and pains becoming more evident with every minute that passed. Her ruined suit went straight into the garbage. Alexa avoided a peek in the mirror. If she looked anything like she felt, her ego couldn't survive that feedback. Unlike being desired by two incredibly sexy men.

Her head thunked against the travertine tile of the luxurious shower's wall as the water heated up. She debated whether the show she'd given downstairs should be classified as the most amazing, or stupidest, thing she'd ever done in her life. The afterglow of her orgasm still diminished the part of her that had been scared to death by the attack earlier but, damn, it complicated things.

Denying her scalding attraction to both brothers would be pointless. Justin's wild, open, adventurous spirit made the ideal counterpoint to Jason's practical, organized, responsible character. All her life, she'd struggled to reconcile her prerequisite for stability with her craving for spontaneity. Together, the brothers could meet her every need. She didn't try to delude herself, Jason's eyes had promised her their experiment downstairs meant more than simple act of kindness or distraction.

No, it was a test. He's smart enough to know I'd freak out, and restrained enough to wait for me to cave.

She shut off the water with a snap of her wrist that sent sparks shooting down her arm. Damn, she'd banged her elbow pretty hard. The bruises sprinkled across her side and around the top of her arm had already begun to darken. She said a silent prayer for Justin's timing as she toweled dry. She would be lying dead in an alley somewhere by now if he hadn't stopped her attacker.

Poor Justin, does he realize that his brother intends to have me too?

She added guilt to the pile of emotions bearing down on her, belted the thick robe around her waist and prepared to find out what the hell was going on.

*****

Justin rejoined his brother after changing his clothes. He grimaced when he imagined Alexa's opinion of his juvenile reaction.

"Don't worry." Jason took one look at him and understood his thoughts. Nothing unusual there, it happened all the time.

"I must have missed the day in health class where they taught that coming in your pants was a recommended method of impressing a woman." He snagged a beer out of the fridge and plopped down on the deep leather couch in the living room just off the kitchen.

"Trust me, she enjoyed it." His brother's voice thickened. "The look on her face…"

"Maybe you should have let it rip in that fancy suit of yours, too. At least you wouldn't be so damn horny now." He laughed at Jason's horrified expression. He would never think of messing up his fine, tailored wardrobe.

"Listen." His twin turned serious. "I want you to know that I didn't do that on purpose. I thought you could kiss her, take her mind off the pain, but things sort of got out of hand."

Hmm, interesting. "Since when am I opposed to sharing my women with you, Jay? Last I checked, I enjoyed it. We both do."

"Alexa isn't some party girl looking for a wild time." Jason got defensive. He leaned forward, setting his soft drink on the coaster protecting the coffee table. He reached one hand back and rubbed his neck.

"No, you're right about that." Jason never acted this uncertain. Justin found it awkward to reassure him. "I wasn't giving her some line before. I think she's amazing."

"Exactly my point. I don't want to ruin what you have going with her. I know you just met her, but this could be the real thing for you. She's different."

"Jay, I may not have several flashy degrees or rule a corporate empire but I'm not a fucking idiot." Before his brother could object, he barreled on. "I *know* this is the real thing. But not just for me, for us both. She's the hottest woman I've ever laid eyes on. That day in the woods... Shit, Jay, I already told you how it was, like I'd die if I couldn't have her. But just now, with you there, it ratcheted things up until I thought she'd start glowing like white-hot metal. Seeing her in that suit made me realize she's not only wild at heart. She lives in both our worlds. She needs us both."

In another rare moment, Justin's discourse rendered Jason speechless. Clearly, he wanted to pursue the matter further but they'd both heard the shower shut off a minute ago. Neither wanted to risk being overheard. Sure enough, light footsteps sounded on the stairway behind them.

He covered for them. "Now, quit stalling and tell me why someone wants to know about your business enough to face felony charges over it."

CHAPTER FIVE

"That's a really good question." Alexa entered the room and faced the brothers. Justin sprawled on the beefy leather couch while Jason sat, with perfect posture, on the elegant wingback chair beside it. The eclectic mix of furniture suited the room.

Justin patted the cushion by his side. "Sit down, you're still pale."

He looked delicious in his faded rock band T-shirt and jogging pants. She couldn't explain why the sight of his masculine bare feet turned her on but the flip of her stomach that resulted grew into a full out lurch when her stare darted away and landed on the hint of smooth, ripped chest that peeked through Jason's button-down shirt. Not to mention the sinewy forearms that rested next to each other as he crossed his arms over his lean stomach.

Everything about them turns you on.

She grabbed a sage microfiber blanket off the opposite arm of the couch and tucked it around her like a shield before settling a safe distance away from Justin. The combination of the central air conditioning and her wet hair made the velvety cover seem rational, though they scalded her with the appetite in their eyes. It also ensured she didn't flash them by accident and cause the whole house to explode from the sexual tension her bare flesh might incite. She needed to gather information without distractions.

"Don't bother trying to shut us down." She could tell Jason was preparing to dodge their questions about the business again. "We're in this together now."

"I've decided this venture is too risky." His face became stony, determined. "I'll spread the word I'm withdrawing my bid."

Justin ignored him and turned to Alexa instead. In a stage whisper he said, "He's lying. Sometimes he goes all big brother on me, since he's a whole two minutes older, like I can't take care of myself."

The thought that Jason considered his six-foot-something, muscled, badass brother in need of his defense inspired a grin but she played along, nodding in sympathy. "He does seem to have that protective streak down."

"But, really, he'll keep working this deal on his own. It's too intriguing for him to pass up." He winked and her insides compressed with longing. "So we'll just wait until he thinks we're not looking and then jump in on our own which will be much riskier than if he'd let us work together in the first place."

Jason rolled his eyes in exasperation. She burst out laughing at the sight of one of the country's most influential businessmen acting like a teenage girl. "Oh, for the love of God. You're not going to quit are you?"

"No." Though Justin acted playful, his emotions ran deep. She read the tension in his whitened knuckles grasping the beer bottle so tight she feared it might crack.

"And neither will I." She committed to helping now, if only to screw the people who had tried to kidnap her. "You offered me a job, and I accept."

Jason's eyes darted between them, weighing his options for a moment, before he stalked into the kitchen and retrieved a steel case. In the confusion earlier, Alexa had assumed it was a briefcase but now she saw it was far too bulky and heavy for that.

He set it on the sturdy coffee table in front of them and snapped open the lid.

She slid closer, enticed by the electronic gizmo inside. Her elbow bumped Justin's when he leaned toward the puzzling object. Circuits made of precious metals glinted, reflecting the halogen can light from overhead.

Justin reached into the case, hesitating a second to peer up at his brother.

"Jay, this isn't what I think it is, is it?" He'd obviously made the leap ahead of her. She recognized a fuel cell and a miniature engine but...that would make the cylinder on the end...

"Wow." She had to concentrate on keeping her mouth closed.

The tiny motor fit comfortably in Justin's hands as he lifted it to examine the modified attachment.

"Exactly." Jason sounded weary. "About three weeks ago, a small research and development start up approached me, claiming to have invented a highly efficient technology powered by a revolutionary biofuel source. They promised their engine ran on renewable, cheap and environmentally friendly fuel. One that could eliminate our reliance on oil and other petroleum products forever. "

"And this is what? A prototype?" Justin tested wires and fittings, he twisted and removed a component.

"Should you be doing that?" The magnitude of change such a technology could bring staggered her. Watching Justin dismantle it without a thought to the consequences set her on edge.

"Yeah, I get engines." He barely paid attention to his response, his focus absorbed in the mechanical parts.

"So do I, but this is unique. Stop. Let's take some pictures first, draw up a diagram…"

He paused to grin up at her. "You're going all Jay on me there, babe."

"Don't worry, Alexa. I documented every detail as soon as they delivered the prototype." Jason smiled down at her in commiseration. "Then I put out word that I was looking to hire a technology consultant. The best of the best."

"So you've had this for weeks and didn't show it to me?" Justin acted pissed but she knew the emotion stemmed from hurt. "I fucking knew something was up with you. Why did you keep denying it?"

"Because you would've wanted to dive right in and I had to do more research first. Then you were...preoccupied." He sighed.

"You did what you thought was best, Jason. You couldn't have known how dangerous the situation would get." Their eyes met and held. She detected regret, longing and, not least of all, desire. The longer they watched each other, the more his gaze heated until Justin interrupted.

"Something's not quite right." He pointed to a gear and hose component. "Here."

"That's the problem." Jason sighed. "It doesn't work. There's an integral component missing."

"How much do they want for it?" Justin pushed back on the couch, the engine abandoned where he laid it on the table.

"Fifty billion." Jason's calm declaration nearly sent her through the roof. Fifty billion dollars. For just one part. Not to mention the cost of R&D, production and marketing. A deal of this magnitude was out of her league, light years beyond even her last project. Jason's faith in selecting her for this position staggered her.

"And I would gladly have raised it. I only wanted to gather a team of experts before word got out. People I could trust. I needed Alexa to head up the program while I was out campaigning for funds and building a consortium to protect our investment. Even Winston Industries can't secure the kind of a bond that will be necessary to develop this on its own."

He beamed at her before continuing. "She's the best in her field. Her reputation, and my research, guaranteed she could handle the political posturing, maintain the level of detail necessary, coordinate all the departments involved and her mechanical capability would allow her to interface with the technical teams, which I hoped to recruit you for. I've been eying her for Winston Industries for some time and this was the golden opportunity. It seemed rational at the time, but you're right to criticize my over planning."

"We're in this together now, Jay. We'll work it out." Justin reassured his brother.

There were no hard feelings but Alexa could tell from Jason's stiff posture that they hadn't heard the whole story yet.

Again, the brothers had an entire subliminal conversation she couldn't quite follow. First, Justin raised his eyebrows. Then Jason shook his head. In response, Justin muttered a curse under his breath.

"What am I missing?" She glanced from one to the other, trying to gauge their expressions.

"The start up's head scientist had a heart attack and died this morning." Jason's cynicism made it clear he didn't believe the fatality a natural death.

"Fuck." Justin scrubbed his fingers through his hair.

"I'm assuming that's when the thieves realized the design had already been shared with Winston Industries and decided to hunt down the details. I'm sorry, Alexa, I didn't know. The message was highly classified and I missed my assistant in the hallway en route to our meeting. I never would have let you leave alone if I'd realized. Once the information leaked, I put us all in jeopardy. I almost got you killed."

Reminded of her narrow escape earlier, she shivered. Her attackers hadn't been playing around. People had been killed for far less than billions of dollars.

"Come here." Before she could protest, Justin tugged her into his lap and surrounded her with his body, which radiated warmth. She could tell he needed to hold her as much as she wanted him to by the desperation in his clutching hands. They were in deeper than she'd ever imagined. "Son of a bitch! We might have lost you before we really knew you."

Her pulse raced. "We?"

"You want us both. Don't you, honey?" Justin trailed his hand down her shoulder, swiping the blanket away from her.

"I..." Her mind still reeled from the revelation of the invention. Switching focus, she thought about what he implied. Could she really be with two men? Sex on the hood of her car had been a serious departure from her comfort zone. This...

"Don't pressure her, Justin." Jason's warning unfroze her. She shook off his concern and decided to be blunt.

"You're okay with sharing?" She couldn't keep the incredulousness from her voice.

"Hell, yes." Justin played with the knot in the terrycloth belt. "Let us show you how good we can make it for you."

His daring didn't surprise her but Jason's slight nod of agreement shocked her. For someone so careful and proper, their proposition shattered logic and promised chaos for ignoring the consequences.

"We're two halves of a whole, Alexa," Jason explained without trying to persuade her. "It's always been this way."

"You've done this before?" she asked, though she suspected the answer.

"Yes," they answered in unison.

Time suspended as Justin's energy crackled, practically stinging her with its restlessness, while Jason's level stare permitted her room to decide. His reserve challenged her more than his twin's exuberance. Experience had taught her that passionate emotions could burn out in a flash but Jason's patient desire coaxed her into a situation that could only result in disaster.

She knew her weaknesses. Falling for the wrong man ranked high on the list. She barely knew these men and already she craved them. What would happen if she let herself care for them?

Jason turned away and said, "She's not ready, Justin."

The stab of disappointment that tore through Alexa convinced her to act before she regretted this moment for the rest of her life.

"Wait." Both sets of green eyes turned on her like lasers. She wiggled off Justin's lap and stood between them. Throwing caution to the wind, she shrugged the bathrobe off her shoulders and let it drop to the floor. She'd never felt as sexy as when they both drew nearer, as though they couldn't resist.

Justin rotated forward and dropped to his knees at her feet in front of the couch. Jason closed the gap between them with one long stride. She shivered when Justin's hands bracketed her hips and his warm lips kissed her reverently just below her belly button. Jason stood close, his chest brushing hers every time she drew another rapid breath. He refrained from touching her when he asked, "You're sure?"

In response, she locked her arms around his solid back and pulled him close, angled to the side so both brothers fit against her. "Yes." She couldn't stop the moan that escaped a moment before she rose up on her tiptoes to place her lips on his in a light kiss. Eyes wide open, she watched desire dilate his pupils when he reciprocated. Kissing Jason was a sweet, intoxicating experience. His fingers supported her neck as he deepened the contact, his tongue nudging her lips, teasing her. Her legs trembled and she might have fallen if not for the two men holding her steady.

Without a word, Jason stepped away, breaking their embrace. She groaned at the loss but, before she could protest further, Justin scooped her into his arms and followed Jason up the stairs, taking them two at a time. They turned into the blue room. Jason peeled the thick comforter out of the way even as Justin leaned forward and placed her in the center of the huge, king-sized bed. The smooth, high thread count sheets cradled her, caressing her skin. Justin followed her down, his mouth surrounding one of her nipples. He licked, laved and nipped her playfully as she watched Jason strip off his clothes.

He didn't hurry. Instead, he unbuttoned the crisp blue shirt with deliberate movements as he observed his brother feasting on her. He studied her reactions while untucking the Oxford and setting it neatly aside, draped over the arm of a nearby chair.

"You like it when he sucks just that way." Jason's words thrilled her. Justin adjusted his technique based on the observation, increasing the waves of pleasure his wet mouth produced. Jason slowly unbuckled his belt. She couldn't take her eyes away from his fingers hovering over the button of his slacks. The material formed an impressive tent where his cock lay hard and aching beneath. Instead of freeing it, he continued to tease her by drawing the leather from around his waist inch by inch.

He coiled it around his fist and the image he made, bare chest gleaming with a light sheen of perspiration, looming over the bed, in complete control caused a spasm to run through her pussy. "Have you ever had a man use a belt on your lush ass before, sweetheart?"

She shook her head before gasping, "No."

The thick, erect length of Justin's cock thumped against her thigh through the soft cotton of his pants as it twitched in response.

"Hmmm," Jason nearly purred. "Maybe next time."

Her nipple hardened further as Justin blew cool air across the damp skin before switching to sweep his tongue across the other breast. The unhurried strip tease continued to torture her. Jason flicked open the button on his slacks and unzipped them before nudging them down his long, muscled legs, leaving him standing in his black boxer briefs, the prominent bulge stretching over nearly to his hip bone. He looked like a picture clipped out of a Playgirl magazine.

Justin trailed his hand down the center of her body, heading straight toward her soaking mound. Her back arched as she tried to direct herself closer to his wandering palm. She needed him to touch her, to still the lust his expert manipulation of her flesh and the sight of his brother's hard, six pack abs generated.

"You want him to pet that pretty pussy, don't you?" She writhed beneath Justin's strokes and Jason's infatuated stare.

"Yes. Oh, yes." She couldn't believe the frenzied plea in her voice but, damn, she'd never wanted a man's touch as desperately as she did right now.

Jason pushed his underwear down his thighs, liberating his full hard-on, which bounced heavy against his ripped thigh. A single drop of pearly liquid beaded at the tip and she licked her lips.

Her eyes closed when Justin's fingertip invaded the top of her drenched slit and followed it downward. Her hips bucked at the intensity of that glancing touch, driving the digit further between her swollen lips. Justin licked her stomach as he moved lower, his fingers flitting over the folds of her pussy. When the mattress dipped, her eyes flew open to discover Jason sitting near the top of the bed, his hips angled toward her, his legs extending down her side as he lounged against the headboard. He pillowed her head on his abdomen, stroking her hair, tracing the shell of her ear, smoothing along her eyebrows with one fingertip before brushing it over her mouth.

She opened her lips, sucking it into her mouth on a moan even as Justin's finger snuck just inside the entrance of her tightening channel. Alexa glanced down to see Justin, now naked—his clothes thrown in a hasty pile at the foot of the bed—nestled between her thighs. His broad shoulders spread her legs further apart to accommodate him.

"You smell so good, baby." He buried his face against her skin, inhaling deeply. His desire was organic. Jason's cock jumped at the sight, branding her collarbone with its heat as it bobbed against her. She turned her head from the erotic sight Justin made and reached forward. Jason helped by shifting his body, cradling her head.

"That's right, sweetheart. Go ahead, suck me." He guided her mouth over the engorged tip of his cock. The moment her tongue swiped the tangy fluid from the slit in the head, Justin sank his finger inside her clenching pussy, spreading the rings of muscle to accommodate its broad length.

She moaned when he followed the thrust with his tongue on her clit, causing Jason's cock to slide further into her mouth. Alexa devoured him with eager swallows. Her enthusiasm was rewarded with Jason's groan of approval and the beginning strokes of Justin's finger deep inside her. She palmed Jason's balls in one hand, loving the way they flexed and tightened in her light grasp.

He leaned forward, testing her nipples with firm squeezes that sent shockwaves to her pussy. Justin added another finger, preparing her for his oversized cock. His lips encased her clit with liquid warmth, sliding over the sensitive nub as he gently licked it. Her muscles gathered tension and she drove Jason's cock deeper into her mouth, causing the head to bump against the back of her throat.

"Right there, Justin." Jason's gravelly instruction directed his brother to the perfect spot. "Make her come. Now."

Justin's fingers curved inside her, the pads of his fingers stroking the front wall of her vagina, locating the ultimate pleasure point, trapping it between his skilled fingers and her pubic bone. Sensation overwhelmed her in a tsunami of passion. She came hard around his hand. Her slick juices coated Justin's face as she swallowed Jason's cock in time to the spasms wracking her body. The waves of orgasm lessened but didn't die out within her as Justin continued to wring pleasure from her body.

Jason's harsh breathing penetrated the roaring in her mind but Justin's voice captured her attention.

"I need to fuck you." He dislodged his fingers from the still clutching grasp of her pussy and crawled up her body until he knelt between her thighs and the plump head of his cock lined up with her dripping opening.

Alexa tilted her head just enough to beg around the proud shaft filling her mouth. "Please. Yes."

Justin groaned as his hips thrust forward, burying himself several inches deep inside her. "I can't hold back, honey." He jerked his cock out then rammed into her again, scooting her up to press tight against the muscled wall of his twin's abdomen. He stretched her impossibly, only causing her desire to spike with the edge of pain.

She tasted the salty musk of Jason's precome and knew he was close to surrendering.

"So small, you're stretched tight around him." Jason's rough, broken words spurred her higher and the ripples of her extinguishing orgasm flared to life.

He gave a harsh moan and tried to pull away but she increased her hold on his balls, keeping him in place, right where she wanted him. "No. Justin." The urgency in Jason's voice broke through to his brother, keeping all three of them poised on the razor edge of pleasure when Justin paused his pounding rhythm. "Condom."

Alexa didn't stop worshiping Jason's steel-hard flesh long enough to tell him she took the pill. She just shook her head no as emphatically as she could with his thick cock buried in her throat and flexed her pussy around Justin, encouraging him to deliver what he promised.

"Oh, God. Can't stop." Justin grabbed her ass, tugging her down onto him even as he buried himself as deep as he could get inside her, grinding his pubic bone against her clit. She felt full to bursting as the head of his cock pressed against her cervix. He thrust inside her fully, extracting all the way out before shoving completely inside her again. Once, twice, and then her world erupted in a flood of lights and ecstasy.

Jason's sac tightened in her palm, and the contractions of his body prepared her, moments before jets of hot come scalded her throat and soothed the flaming need in her pussy. Simultaneously, Justin pumped his seed deep inside her, calling out her name over and over as Jason fed her his own ardor.

She greedily swallowed one last time and whimpered at the hollow sensation left behind when Jason's cock slipped from her lips. He glided down her body, grabbing the comforter from the foot of the bed. He turned her onto her side and gathered her close, her back to him even as Justin pivoted to lie in front of her, still locked deep.

The blanket settled over them and she drifted off to sleep, exhausted from adrenaline and spent passion. Their hands stroked her mindlessly, her aches and pains long forgotten, thoughts of lurking danger banished by the two men bracketing her.

They would keep her safe and satisfied.

CHAPTER SIX

Alexa surfaced in stages from a sound sleep. Bobbing into consciousness, she became aware of shreds of reality each time she struggled to open her eyes but lost out to the utter relaxation sedating her. First, she noted her bed felt luxurious and more comfortable than she remembered. Next, she sighed and nuzzled closer to the warm, firm body nearby. Finally, enough awareness returned to allow her to chastise herself for the wild abandon of the night before.

She bolstered her nerve and peeked out from under heavy lids at the tousled, sexy man lounging on his side, elbow propped in hand, monitoring her rest.

"Morning sunshine." His lazy, smug voice spoke of his absolute contentment.

"Mmm. Justin." She hadn't intended for her reply to sound so welcoming but truth outpaced her instinctive denial of enjoying such a taboo affair. She had loved every minute of the night before and couldn't wait to do it again.

He reached out, stroking the side of her face as she lay next to him on her back, her head propped up on his sculpted biceps. The tenderness in his eyes swamped her and she started to retreat. Smoking hot sex was one thing, but affection from a man like this could be fatal to her heart.

"Shhh. Lay here a minute more with me." His free arm snaked around her waist, pinning her to the ultra-plush mattress. "Jay is downstairs making some food to bring you in bed. You wouldn't want to spoil his surprise, would you?"

Her stomach growled and she relaxed beneath him, defeated. It would be impossible to argue since she wanted to soak in the moment. Jason's thoughtfulness touched her. Of course he realized she'd be starving. They hadn't eaten dinner last night. He probably even deduced that her nerves had prevented her from eating lunch before the big meeting yesterday. Breakfast sounded heavenly.

"How are you feeling this morning?" Concern replaced the affection in his expression. That she could handle. Alexa stretched, testing her muscles with tentative movements. She winced when the stiffness in her ribs and leg penetrated the lingering haze of waking.

"Not too bad," she lied.

Justin lifted the thick down comforter away from her in stages. He paused to inspect the bruises ringing her upper arm first. He bent over her, pressing a soft kiss just beneath the obvious finger marks.

"Poor baby." He grunted as he tugged the quilted blanket to her waist and saw the discolored flesh stretching over her ribcage. It must have looked pretty nasty because his attention didn't waver from the injury to her fully bared breasts. He trailed his fingertips over the area, light enough to tickle a bit, before taking his hand away and touching his lips to his palm. Justin laid it over her side in a gesture that melted her further.

He made his way down to the top of her thigh where a trimmed bandage smacking of Jason's attention to detail covered the neat row of stitches. His hand trembled when he traced the outline of the gauze.

His attention snapped up to her face. "I'm sorry I wasn't more careful with you last night. Did I hurt you?"

"No." She shook her head, she hadn't felt pain, only pleasure. But if he hadn't shown up when he did...

"I just wish I'd gotten there sooner." Regret marked his features before simmering anger covered it over. "If I find the bastard that did this to you, he's dead."

"I never said thank you," she whispered.

Justin leaned forward until his forehead rested against hers and avoiding his gaze became impossible. "You could thank me now."

The steamy look accompanying his words dared her to ask, "What did you have in mind?"

His broad smile betrayed his trickery and she anticipated a naughty request. "I want to know why you ran from me that day in the mountains. Why you're still running now."

"Are you sure you wouldn't rather have a blow job?" she bargained.

"Very tempting." He chuckled at her audacity. "But I need to understand what's holding you back."

"The fact that I slept with two men at once last night isn't enough?" She hoped her attitude masked her vulnerability. She teetered off balance, torn between the strength of her emotions for two men, practically strangers, and her logical conclusion that nothing lasting could come of the situation.

"Honey, you can lie to yourself, but you can't fool me. I tasted your desire when it flooded my mouth." She couldn't deny it. "You loved every moment of it."

"That doesn't mean that I think it was prudent." She fought to keep herself cold and rational. Pushing up from the bed, she tried to escape but Justin wouldn't allow it. He snagged her wrist and returned her to her place beside him.

"It wasn't prudent to let me come inside your hot pussy without protection?" He thought the lack of a condom bothered her. "I swear I've never done that before. I'm sorry, we should have talked about it first but, for the record, I'm healthy."

"I'm on the pill. My *body* is safe." She worried about her heart.

"Someone hurt you." His scrutiny cut too deep for her comfort. "Worse than these bruises."

Tears stung her eyes as she frantically tried to blink them away. She wanted to slap him with her words, gain some space to think. "Just like you will, too."

He didn't even flinch. "It's not going to happen, babe. You can trust us."

"I know your type, Justin." She couldn't keep the bitterness from her voice. "You're reckless, fickle, unfaithful and commitment phobic."

"No, darlin'." The volume of his retort escalated. "You're the one who's afraid, not me. I'm willing to admit that I've fallen head over heels for you. You want to hear me say it? Fine. I. Love. You. And that's not going to change."

"What? That's crazy! I just met you!" She lurched in an attempt to jump up but collapsed gasping and pushing a hand against her ribs. The gesture granted him a reprieve from the tirade she prepared to launch.

"It's fucking true! The world feels right when I'm with you. I don't need a year or ten to know that I'll never find a woman like you again. I won't throw that away because you're scared."

"Yelling in her face probably isn't the best approach to convince her of what little self-control you possess." Jason's deadpan delivery came from the doorway in an attempt to diffuse the situation but Alexa lay stunned by the impact of Justin's words and emotions.

He scrubbed his hands over his face. "Shit. You're right, that was...stupid."

The shrill ringing of the house phone drowned out his last syllable. Both brothers stiffened, becoming instantly alert. Jason set the tray he carried on the bed and grabbed for the receiver on the nightstand.

Angling closer, Justin whispered in her ear as Jason punched the talk button. "Only a few emergency contacts have access to that number."

"Hello?" Tension emanated from each stiff muscle in Jason's body. "I see. Yes. We'll be there." He replaced the handset in the cradle with a precise snap of his wrist.

"When and where, Jay?" Justin asked as though he'd heard the conversation himself.

"You have to stop doing that!" She squirmed from beneath him and faced them with hands on hips, unconcerned by her nakedness. "What the hell was that about?"

"Seems someone from the R&D lab kept process notes and they're willing to make a deal." Jason looked between her and Justin in silent communication but this time she understood exactly what they intended.

"Oh, no you don't." She stepped between them, cutting off their line of sight. "I'm going too."

***

Justin watched his brother cross the gloomy street in front of their parked car. The tinted glass made surveillance possible, hiding them from any onlookers. The caller had demanded Jason come alone but neither he nor Alexa would have permitted a solo excursion. He hoped the fact they refrained from calling the cops would satisfy the informant.

"Son of a bitch," he muttered under his breath as Alexa unfolded her lithe body from the backseat and climbed upfront. The awkward position must have hurt like hell considering her injuries but it gave him a world-class view of her luscious behind.

"Are you looking at my ass?" Her scathing tone implied he better not be.

"Yup."

"How about you watch out for Jason instead?" She had a point there. He swiveled his head to face out the windshield. Although his brother trained in self defense to protect against money seeking schemers, it never hurt to have help.

"How did you talk us into letting you get involved in this again?" Justin fired the words from where he fumed in the passenger seat.

"I was already involved, remember?" Like he could forget the horror of witnessing her half-jammed into the hatch of that van. "Besides, no matter what he thinks, Jason needs someone to cover his ass while he's exposed out there. From the way you're holding that gun I assume you actually know how to use it, but it probably requires some concentration. In addition, you couldn't refute that it would be easier to protect him if someone else were in charge of the exit plan. I happen to be an excellent driver. Plus, I'm an even better negotiator. It's one of the reasons Jason hired me in the first place."

"I'll keep that in mind." The sly smile she sent him caused his cock to harden, a distraction he couldn't afford right now. He had to clarify one thing, though, in case this situation went to shit like his instincts screamed it would.

"About what I said...you know, before." Justin cleared his throat while keeping his attention glued to the surroundings, monitoring every nook and cranny of the shadowed alley for signs of trouble.

"Don't worry about it." Alexa attempted to brush him off. "Lots of people say things in the heat of the moment they don't mean."

Huh?

He heard her fidgeting, fingers toying with the zipper on her purse as she removed something metallic from inside and fiddled around with it. He risked a glance in her direction and caught the uncertain expression she wore as she chewed on her moist bottom lip. He nearly groaned.

Eyes forward, chief.

Jason stood with his back to a brick wall, vigilant, awaiting his contact's arrival.

"You have it all wrong." How could he do anything but love her? She was sweet, sexy, brave, smart, daring and a perfect fit for both him and his twin. "I want to apologize for the way I told you. I know you're not ready to deal with it yet. I'm not going to rush you. I just wanted you to know I'm not fucking around here."

He paused for a moment, double checking their surroundings. Her unusual silence urged him to continue. Maybe she would actually listen.

"Look, I don't know what that jackass did to you..."

She interrupted. "He promised to love me forever but he really meant until he got bored. I walked in on him with the next gullible woman he met."

Justin snuck a glimpse at their woman. Her curt explanation didn't obscure the agony in her beautiful eyes but it did demonstrate how she had evolved to protect herself, by controlling her emotions and playing things safe. When a woman like Alexa loved, her whole soul would be exposed with nothing held in reserve. Giving that trust, and having it betrayed, had scarred her heart.

He was determined to heal it.

"Damn, honey. I can't say I'm sorry 'cause if he wasn't a supreme fool, you wouldn't be here now. I'll never let go of what we have but I'll try to give you room to accept it. I'll be right here waiting for you to tell me you're ready. That's a promise."

He cursed his timing when a lone figure in a black trench coat approached, preventing her from responding. The man's innocuous appearance contradicted Justin's expectations for the bearer of information that had already cost the life of one person. His average height, plain brown hair and nondescript form helped him avoid attracting attention as he made his way in front of the car.

Justin's fingers tightened on the grip of the S&W he held at the ready when the stranger's hand dipped into the front pocket of his long coat. He relaxed marginally when the man retrieved a manila envelope instead of the weapon Justin feared. Maybe they'd get the info and get out of here quick and painlessly after all.

***

Jason prepared himself to knock the newcomer over and bolt for the car if he so much as looked at Jason funny, confident that Justin would have him covered. He wanted to stay and force some answers from the man but he wouldn't risk Alexa's safety by keeping her out in the open any longer than necessary. The thought of losing her had already become unbearable. As crazy as it seemed, Justin's bold declaration this morning had been the truth. A better partner for them didn't exist.

The man barely made it up to him before he dug inside his coat and flipped out a packet of papers. "Take them. Hurry, I'm being followed." The strained words accompanied a paranoid glance behind him as though someone might be standing right over his shoulder.

Jason held out a wad of money, the amount specified for the trade.

"Keep it. I just want to get out of the game." He spun on his heels and headed off.

For one split second, Jason considered inviting the man to the sanctuary of their house but he couldn't risk a trap. Not with Alexa involved.

"Thank you," Jason called to the retreating form.

The brisk footsteps paused as he turned back, nodding stiffly, a moment before his face froze in a grimace of shocked pain and a red stain blossomed across his forehead.

"Oh fuck!" Jason rushed to the spot where the man had collapsed but his eyes already glazed, his limbs folded, completely lax, in a unique state reserved for death.

A distant corner of his mind registered the car screeching up to the curb and the telltale ping of a bullet ricocheting off the pavement near his feet before Justin's shout rang out.

"Let's go, it's too late for him." Then, a second later, "Jason! Move it, now!"

Jason stumbled to the car waiting open for him and slid inside. Justin reached through the open window to slam the door shut with one hand while firing a few shots at a target Jason couldn't see.

The memory of the stricken informant obscured everything else.

CHAPTER SEVEN

lexa set her iPod on the center console, thankful that Jason had arranged to have someone grab a few essentials from her apartment last night. She attached the cables to the car stereo a moment before all hell broke loose. Justin shouted at her to pull forward, Jason stumbled back into the car and shots echoed with an eerie whine when Justin returned fire on an unseen assailant. She slammed the stick in gear and peeled away. Filtering all distractions from her mind, she focused on the job at hand.

Rounding the corner, she forced her muscles to relax and let years of training take over. "Turn on the music," she instructed Justin without removing her eyes from the road flying by faster with every gear change.

"Holy shit, now is not the time!" He spun around, scouting out the road behind them. "There are two black sedans and a motorcycle in pursuit."

She waited for him to finish reloading the gun before reiterating. "Press the dial at 6 o'clock and hang on."

Avoiding a semi, she tucked them into a space barely larger than the car itself. Justin's shoulder slammed against the door, resulting in additional cursing.

"Sit down, put your belt on and play my damn music!" Her command left no room for argument. He settled himself as she wove into the current of traffic on the highway, avoiding another injury.

"Not like I can keep a steady line now anyway." He grumbled before flipping down the mirrored visor to check on Jason. "You are okay, aren't you?"

"Yeah." Jason's monotone response reached them.

"Alexa, step on it, they're still right behind us."

She observed the vehicles in her rear and side view mirrors, aware of their exact positions. "Turn it on."

"Jesus Christ, you're stubborn. Fine. Here." He stabbed the button harder than necessary, the result of too much adrenaline, and the heavy beat of her selected score enveloped them.

She always accompanied her drives with music. It helped her get lost in the rhythm of the lines blazing by and focus on the opportunities between the drivers she streaked past. She edged ahead within moments, taking carefully weighed chances. She calculated each turn, pass and merge before accepting the risk.

Beside her, Justin whooped with her successful movements, each increasing the distance between them and their tails. His enthusiasm faded to the background as the song transformed into a precise staccato refrain. She evaluated her options and studied the pattern of traffic before ditching from the highway at the last safe moment to exit onto an industrial strip of road. Warehouses lined the narrow street and huge trucks transporting goods abounded.

Only the biker remained behind them.

The skilled rider had the advantage, his motorcycle faster and more agile than Jason's sedan, though Justin had obviously worked his magic on the car at some point. It responded with a roar when she needed power and accelerated quicker than she expected. Still, her chance to get away lay in being a smarter driver.

"What time is it?" She spoke in a calm, even tone.

"Time to go home," Jason protested from behind her and she risked a quick glance at him. His pale face glowed against the dark leather interior and he gripped the oh-shit handle in the door hard enough that it would bear permanent dents.

Thank God he's okay. Her heart shuddered when she reflected on what might have happened, causing her to lose focus for a moment.

"Watch out!" Justin's warning swung her attention back to the road in front of her where she avoided a parked car with inches to spare.

She accelerated, bringing them up to speed, regaining her composure with fluid grace.

"Who set the clock in this car?" She asked. When Jason grunted a response, she counted on it being exact. "The time?"

"Five thirty-three." Justin didn't bother asking why anymore.

While they'd waited for the doomed man to deliver his notes to Jason, she'd spent her time plotting. She traveled a route parallel to this road on her way home from the office on good weather nights, when she used an evening tour to unwind. Nothing ruined a drive in her convertible faster than being stuck in miles of traffic, choking on exhaust fumes. Therefore, she tracked most of the possible pitfalls in the city.

She nodded. "We'll make it."

"What are you doing?" Jason's censure shone through.

"Taking you home, safe and sound." She navigated on autopilot, maneuvering the vehicle with efficient tactics. She managed to sneak away from the motorcycle at times but he always caught up again. She didn't have a choice.

"Time?" Alexa checked her speed, too.

"Five thirty-six." Justin read off the glowing numbers. "You have a plan?"

"Yeah but we're too early." She swung out wide and doubled back on their path, heading straight toward the man on the bike. He dodged out of their trajectory, expecting her to attempt to ram him but she couldn't do that.

"Tell me when the clock turns to five thirty-eight." She continued to backtrack until Justin gave her the signal.

"Now."

As soon as the road cleared, she swung the car around one hundred and eighty degrees with a screech of tires to finish the loop.

"Five thirty-nine," Justin announced. "But he's still there, about five hundred feet behind us."

Perfect.

She came over the ridge on West Hamilton and Jason shouted from the backseat. "You're not going to..."

Alexa judged the gap sufficient and committed to the stunt, slamming the gas pedal to the floor.

"Wahoo!" Justin howled as they dove into the center ghost island, around the stopped cars, and flew across the tracks in front of the five forty train from downtown. The bike had no choice but to stop or be flattened.

Either way, he couldn't follow.

***

Justin laughed as he whirled her around in circles across the middle of the living room floor. "Fucking brilliant."

Then he ensnared her with a fierce kiss, letting his relief infuse the gesture. Dizziness swamped her senses, but not as a result of being spun. He left her craving his touch when he separated their mouths. He brought his lips close to her ear and whispered, "I need you to take care of Jay for a while."

She nodded.

He lowered her feet to the floor, rubbing her body down every inch of his muscled front along the way, before facing Jason. He sat, still as a statue, in his usual chair with his head buried in his hands, his fingers locked over his fine hair, rumpled for the first time since she'd met him.

"Jay, I'm going to the shop to get some tools. We'll need them if we're going to crack those notes and file a patent on the engine."

Alexa read between the lines. They would only be out of danger once others couldn't profit from the secret.

"It's not safe." Jason's answer sounded hollow.

"No one knows about the second entrance to the house, it's secure."

Even Jason couldn't argue that point. "Don't do anything crazy."

Justin clapped a hand over Jason's shoulder. She witnessed the compassion in Justin's eyes before he turned to go.

When the door shut with a quiet snick, she crossed to Jason. She couldn't bear the sight of his suffering a moment longer. She understood him well enough to grasp the problem he faced. That insight highlighted the seriousness of the affection growing inside her. She'd never experienced such a deep, instinctive bond with anyone before these two incredible men.

She sank to her knees between his feet and laid her head in his lap. "It's not your fault, there's nothing you could have done."

Alexa stroked his leg, surprised to feel him shaking beneath her touch. "I almost invited him to come here, with us. He would have been safe." Jason drew a deep breath. "He didn't even take the money."

"You couldn't have known he was legitimate." She needed to ease his suffering.

His hands slid down from behind his head to settle in her hair. He rubbed it between his fingers, soothing himself by touching her.

"I should have thought to provide him protection." His disappointment and fury radiated through the rigidity of his body.

"You're not superman." She peered up at him, meeting his liquid green gaze. His pain nearly broke her heart.

Oh no, it can't be. I can't care that much. The sudden realization burst free from her soul and she evaluated it with brutal honesty. She did care, and she would give him whatever he needed even if this primal side of him frightened her a little. "Sometimes, we have to take calculated risks."

The fire in his expression singed her, but he still wouldn't accept the solace she offered.

"Take me, Jason." He wavered on the edge of his control, his hand fisting in her hair. "I'm yours, too. We're not only connected because of Justin."

"You don't understand what you're doing." His breath came harsh and uneven. "Don't tempt me. Not now."

A darkness he kept under wraps with sheer force of will seeped through the cracks in his resolve, weakened by the strain of the day. Alexa yearned to discover what the intensity of his emotions would feel like swirling around her. She anticipated his need to regain control and accepted the burden, even at the risk of sacrificing her own.

"Use me." She trusted implicitly that he would not harm her. That bone-deep knowledge provided the freedom to explore the source of the struggle within him. "I want to help. You can't keep this bottled inside."

He drew a harsh breath and scrunched his eyes as though offering up a silent prayer. "Our first time alone should be gentle and romantic. I can't give you that right now."

"That's not what I want." She stood and tugged on his hand. "Please."

His control fractured. Jason lunged from the chair, shoving her in front of him until her back bumped up against the side of the stairwell. He groaned and buried his fingers in her hair. "Last chance, sweetheart." His lips hovered a hairsbreadth from hers.

"Do it." Alexa surged forward, closing the gap between them.

His touch enveloped her. His hands flew over her, unsnapping her jeans as his mouth plundered, stealing her breath through his kiss. They turned, banging their way up the stairs, one or the other pinned against the wall as they stripped clothes away, never breaking contact for more than a moment.

By the time they made it to the top of the stairs, she had wrapped her legs around his waist. Her bare pussy, slick with arousal, slid against the smooth skin of his lower abdomen. His hard-on nestled against her ass while he walked them down the hall to his room. He kicked open the door and deposited her on the cool black satin sheets of the large, artistic, wrought-iron bed. She didn't waste time examining his space but the overall ambiance impressed luxury on her senses.

He came over her on the bed, his hard cock nudging between her legs, and reclaimed her mouth with an animal grace. She wrapped her arms around his powerful back, delighting in the flex and ripple of the muscles there.

Where sex with Justin was playful, Jason's intensity made her feel delicate and oh-so-willing to submit to his inherent domination. Her legs locked around his waist and she attempted to use her heels on his tight ass to urge him inside her, testing him, goading him.

He didn't disappoint.

Jason shook off her efforts, breaking free of her grasp. He deprived her of his touch and the loss caused a physical ache.

"You gave me control." The fire in his eyes set off another wave of desire inside her and she writhed on the mattress beneath his measuring stare.

"Yes, whatever you want," she practically begged.

He climbed from the bed and her attention caught on the sight of his magnificent cock waving in stiff bobs as he crossed the room to his closet in two steps. He retrieved a handful of silk ties and a small leather chest that he placed at the foot of the bed.

With careful deliberation, he knelt at her feet and yanked her ankles apart. The movement shocked her, making her exposure complete. The thrill that rushed through her left no doubt as to how much she loved it and wanted to continue this game.

"You like this?" His gravelly question required no answer but the moan slipped out of her throat anyway.

His strong grip collared each ankle, making them appear dainty in comparison. Jason bent low to brush a kiss over each one before selecting an expensive-looking tie from the pile. He lifted her right ankle, winding the material comfortably, but inescapably, around it before securing the ends to a loop of metal camouflaged by the ironwork in a convenient spot at the corner of the bedframe.

He caught her glance and resolved her curiosity while binding her other leg. "Yeah, it's custom made."

Alexa tested the strength of the knot work and found it secure. She couldn't break free. Unbidden, she whimpered and squirmed on the silky sheets. Every tactile stimulation inflamed nerve endings sensitive to the touch. With her feet immobilized, he slithered up her body, the two remaining ties in hand.

"So beautiful." He trailed the strips over her legs and abdomen.

She arched her hips, trying to reach the dangling fabric with her clit, which throbbed, desperate for attention.

"Not yet." His stern command stilled her attempts and she watched, fascinated as he dropped his head between her legs. His mouth teased her, staying out of reach. "You're so wet, you're spilling your desire on my sheets."

"I'm sorry." She tried to lift her ass off the bed but he delivered a light slap to the inside of her thigh.

"Never apologize for your passion. It's one of the things I love most about you." The declaration startled Alexa but his direct eye contact left no room for deception. His honesty caused her channel to clench and squeeze out more of her fluids. He stooped lower and licked the dampness from the material between her legs. After cleaning the spot, he turned his head and nipped her.

"Please, Jason, hurry." She reached down and attempted to position his head closer, but he refused to budge. "I need you to touch me. Fuck me. Anything. Please."

With a growl, he lurched up and pinned her wrists to the pillow beside her head. Every inch of his body molded tight to her as she panted beneath him. He licked and kissed his way up her throat before slanting his lips over her mouth. His finesse transformed into pure desire as he sucked on her tongue.

She lost herself in the journey he led her on, stealing her sanity as his wet warmth took her mouth. When he pulled away, she resurfaced only to find her wrists bound to each other and the headboard. She struggled a moment, a brief flash of panic setting in before he soothed her with a kiss and a promise.

"You're going to like this. I'll take care of you."

He yanked two pillows from the side of the bed and tucked them beneath her hips, angling them upward. He towered over her. A web of veins, which pulsed in time to his pounding heart, decorated the bulging muscles of his arms and neck, announcing his command over the passion and strength flowing through them. A bead of precome rolled down the head of his cock and dripped a few inches above her pussy. She felt so hot she expected to see it sizzle on her skin.

"Oh God. Please." She couldn't still her body as it undulated beneath him.

"Patience, love." His wide hand smeared the glistening drop across her belly, massaging it into her skin. Nothing in her life had ever been so erotic as this moment.

He turned to the chest she'd all but forgotten and raised the lid. She strained her neck, trying for a glimpse of the contents, but no matter how she struggled, she couldn't see what mysteries the box held. She heard the crumple of packaging opened for the first time a moment before he swung around with a feral gleam in his emerald eyes.

"You've never taken a man in your ass, have you, Alexa?" Her attention flitted between his straining cock, the perspiration dampened muscles of his smooth chest and six pack abs. So focused on his form, she almost missed the question entirely.

"No, never." But she wasn't clueless. If she stayed with the brothers, it would happen sooner or later.

Jason tipped forward, supporting himself on one forearm while the other rested at her hip. He whispered in her ear. "I'm going to prepare you for us. It will hurt less if you cooperate."

She couldn't still her reflexive jerk when the cool, blunt tip of a toy pressed against the opening of her pussy. She bucked beneath him, increasing the contact of their bodies, trying to force it in deeper. He let her have her way this time.

"That's it, sweetheart." His voice rasped in her ear as he teased it with his tongue. "Get it good and wet."

His head lowered to suckle the tip of her breast, alternating broad licks with the sharp edges of his teeth on her nipple. Her pussy contracted so tight the bulbous rubber object squeezed from her grip. She moaned at the loss.

"You want it back?" He dared her to ask for it.

A tremor ran through her entire body at the raw sensuality bursting from him.

"Yes."

He pressed the lubricated tip against her asshole, drenched from the arousal that ran down her crack from her weeping pussy. The bite of discomfort only spurred her higher but instinct caused her to fight the intrusion and the bonds holding her in place. Her head thrashed on the pillow as Jason forced the toy to invade her with steady pressure. He crooned reassurance and pet her hair until the base nestled against her ass, the toy fully seated inside her.

His cock rode her thigh when he buried his face in the crook of her neck, holding her until the sting faded and arousal took its place. "You have no idea how badly I need you."

"And I, you," she promised. Both spoke of more than the psychical.

Some of the desperation seemed to drain from him as he nuzzled her. He lifted his head just enough to fit his mouth over hers. His kiss suffused her with gentle heat that, when combined with the pressure of the object spreading her anus, threatened to make her come apart.

The forbidden act increased her excitement, multiplying the desire inside her.

Finally, his hands framed her face as the heavy head of his cock fit against the entrance to her pussy. Her labia hugged around him, inviting him in. He rocked against her with miniscule movements that began to nudge apart the tight rings of muscle.

"I need all of you, Jason." Instead, the ties restricted her movement, leaving her at his mercy, unable to force him deeper.

"Not yet, sweetheart," he whispered in her ear. "You're going to come so hard around me. I can't wait to feel your wet pussy sucking at my cock. You're so petite , it's going to take a while for me to open you to all of me with that toy in your ass."

His fingers flexed restlessly as his hips continued their relentless torture, driving his shaft a tiny bit deeper with each pass. His cock rubbed and teased the thin wall of flesh separating it from the plug. The sensation triggered a response in nerve endings she never knew existed before. She wondered what it would feel like to have Justin buried deep inside her.

"That's right, Alexa." His hips thrust harder as the same thought occurred to him and spurred him on. "Imagine what it will be like with both of us fucking you."

"Oh God." Her orgasm spiraled closer as his pelvis began to stroke her clit. "I'm going to come."

He froze, leaving her dangling on the edge of oblivion.

"Not until I tell you to." His piercing stare promised her it would be worth the wait.

He began to move again, almost halfway inside her now, and she already felt full to capacity. Her tissue stretched and accommodated him gradually. The waves of pleasure built again.

"Jason." Her moan was ragged. "Can't wait. Need to come."

He pulled back once more before ramming inside her. His cock reached impossibly deep, drawing a gasp as her back arched in astonishment. His balls slapped against the base of the toy in her ass, sending shockwaves up her spine. She tried to suppress the sensations pushing her toward a gigantic release but he noticed and let her off the hook.

"Come for me, Alexa." His command sent her flying. Jason rode through the spasms of her climax, extending the explosion of passion that threatened to overwhelm her.

He fucked her hard, deep and fast until the pulsing pleasure rose again. Her head swished from side to side, trying to escape the intensity radiating from their joining. The wild grunts and moans of Jason's impending orgasm, coupled with the sliding action of his body pressed tight against her clit, threw her into another round of contractions.

"Yes," he moaned. "Milk my cock."

She did just that, clamping around him in rhythmic pulses until she heard him shout her name. The searing heat of his come filled her as he gave her all the pent up need and emotion raging inside him.

CHAPTER EIGHT

lexa slunk down the stairs in search of Justin. She grabbed the handrail to steady her liquefied muscles. Following her earth shattering release, Jason had tended to her, untying her and carrying her to the shower. The calm after the storm of passion they'd shared allowed her time to consider the ramifications of their actions.

The etiquette of a relationship like this escaped her. Would Justin be angry? Had she cheated on him? Uncertainty and fear festered inside her with each passing moment. Although Jason acted like nothing depraved had happened and certainly he wouldn't intentionally hurt his brother, she needed Justin to confirm it. Her confidence in her actions dissipated with each passing moment. Had desire colored her judgment?

She'd excused herself from Jason's sophisticated, dark-wood paneled office where he researched the startup that had originally contacted him, kicking off this chain reaction of disaster. She intended to wait in Justin's workshop for his return. Then, she could confess what they'd done and beg for his forgiveness if he didn't approve.

If only it hadn't felt so right.

She made her way through the kitchen toward the space Jason had indicated adjoined the garage. Light spilled from beneath the door and, as she drew nearer, she heard the pounding rhythm of hard rock music accompanied by the whir of a power tool.

Her pulse skittered when she considered Justin's reaction. He might see her betrayal as grounds to call off their developing relationship. Her sweaty palms and the sinking dread in the pit of her stomach convinced her that the attachment she had to both men transcended simple desire. True, she craved their touch, had become addicted to the potent sexuality they embodied but, more than that, they captured her soul. Being with them was like finding a piece of herself she hadn't realized was missing.

She laid a hand on the door, frozen for a moment, before gathering her courage and shoving it open.

As though he sensed her presence, Justin pivoted when she entered. He clicked off the buffer he used to smooth a chunk of metal while she took stock of the workshop. Clamps, rulers, bits, blades and various accessories lined the walls. Tool chests bursting with supplies sat in each corner and machines ringed a huge raised bench table.

"Exactly what did you need that you didn't already have two of in here?" Her foot tapped the smooth concrete and her arms crossed over her chest as she declared shenanigans.

"Uh...alright, busted." He shook his head ruefully. "I just checked the perimeter with a walk around the house to give you and Jay some time to come to your senses and realize that a good, hard fuck was the best way to work out all your leftover stress. It was driving me crazy. I need to concentrate on this without a major distraction hanging over my head."

"Wait. You *wanted* us to do it?" Some of her uneasiness seeped out. "Without you?"

His smile lit up the room. "You needed it almost as bad as Jay." Then he turned serious. "Look, he's never taken a woman he understood or connected with before. Sure, we slept with women, probably more than was wise. But they were never a serious thing. They were party girls, looking for a fun time. You're the only woman who's ever tempted him to love or challenged his self-control. And by the looks of you, it suits you both."

Justin stalked closer, taking her hand in his own tender grasp. He brought it to his lips and kissed the red lines decorating her wrists like bracelets.

"You enjoyed this?" he asked with genuine curiosity.

Alexa shivered and nodded.

"And this?" He brushed his mouth over the dark spot on her neck she'd glimpsed in the bathroom mirror when Jason toweled her dry earlier.

"God, yes." Admitting it caused a blush to crawl over her face. She attempted to regain influence by focusing on her anger. "But how was I to know you approved?"

He tugged her into his arms, cradling her against his chest. She listened to his steady heartbeat and relaxed.

"I'm sorry, honey. I didn't mean to upset you." He settled his chin on top of her head. "You didn't do anything wrong."

He cupped her shoulders in his hands and braced her. "Hey, look at me, baby." The tenderness in his eyes warmed her heart instead of frightening her this time. "I'm even more thrilled for you and Jay than I am for myself. You're the two people I love most in the world. Whether I'm there or not, you should do what feels right with him. I know he would say the same. You belong with us."

They embraced for a long minute, neither having to speak. He ended the silence when awkwardness infiltrated her for not reciprocating his declarations. Justin didn't pressure her for more than she could give.

"Come on." He led her over to the component he'd been working on when she came in. "I need some help."

***

Jason clicked the print button, sending the last of the supplier documents to the queue. He supplemented business acumen with expert research skills, enabling him to make strategic decisions. Over the years, he'd learned to double check information provided by prospective partners who targeted his successful firm for scams.

Before things went to hell in a hand basket, he'd intended to hire Alexa as the program manager of the new operation. A large part of her position would be to act as a liaison who could decipher the technical specifications and translate them into terms he could understand. She often performed a similar function in her role as a top consultant in the field.

His file on her proved her commitment to her career. She spent months working high intensity projects with ridiculous, long hours. On call, she had to be available 24/7 to extinguish any fires that popped up related to an initiative. Analyzing the information he now possessed would be second nature to her.

Jason straightened the papers, whistling a cheesy song as he made his way out to Justin's workshop. The racket of metal and gears floating up to his bedroom earlier had clued him in to his brother's ruse even if Alexa had been too preoccupied to noticed. He nudged open the door so he could steal a look inside undetected. He scoffed at his own silliness. He'd never craved a simple glimpse of a woman before, but a man in love for the first time wanted to savor every moment.

Alexa perched on a high stool, tinkering with random parts that made little sense to him. Close behind her, Justin stood relaxed, watching over her shoulder, one arm wrapped casually around her waist as they collaborated on a solution.

Jason wondered how he could have known of her all these years and never realized she would be the perfect woman for them. Her profile hadn't captured the adventurous part of her spirit and the chemistry between them had remained untested since he avoided public appearances.

So much time wasted.

He entered the room, making his way toward them. Their ability to concentrate with the radio blasting baffled him. Together, they turned and Alexa's face reflected the same joy he experienced on reuniting with her after their brief separation. Her eyes smoldered with remnants of heat from their earlier interlude. Her submission thrilled him with its beauty and intrinsic trust.

Her protection was a responsibility he took seriously. If they could crack the secret and apply for a patent, their safety would be assured. Only once they eliminated the possibility of someone else profiting from the invention would they be free to continue their lives in peace. Even if they gave up pursuing the engine design, they'd be at risk. Some crazy person might not believe the final piece of the puzzle eluded them.

Suddenly, he wanted to finish this deal and get to the truly important part of his future. Just a few days ago, he'd have sworn the biofuel engine was the most significant development in his life but one sassy woman had changed his mind.

"What do you have, Jay?" Justin's concerned grimace and insightful stare made it clear he shared the same train of thought.

"A present." Jason pressed a quick peck to Alexa's cheek as he set the documents down in front of her. More than a glancing touch and they wouldn't get any work done.

She rifled through the stack to get a sense of the information. On the third or fourth page she paused.

"Why didn't I think of this?" She spoke to herself, engrossed in the data. Ignoring Justin's bewildered look as he tried to interpret the rows of numbers, she began to organize the sheets into piles. She continued to talk to herself.

"We already know what that was for." She crumpled one of the papers and tossed it into a heap of scrap metal that appeared to be bungled attempts at replicating the component.

"No." She added another wad to the trash. "Nope. Got that one. Not it." Garbage. Garbage. Garbage.

"I take it things haven't been going well down here?" Jason raised an eyebrow at his brother.

"Using the notes, we were able to recreate all but one critical piece of the component." He sighed. "We thought we had it but it looks like our friend trusted no one. For the vital connection he removed the full details of the materials used and replaced them with some kind of code. CP. We tried copper pipe, chrome plates, chipped platinum and any other conductors we could think of but, so far…" He shrugged wearily.

Alexa swiveled around, displaying an invoice so they could read it. The letterhead stated *Chastal Partners—your source for fine specialty metals*. Below that, a quantity of one sat beside a single line item—*half-inch gold conduit.*

"Tell me you have some," she pleaded.

Justin yanked open a drawer. Things rattled and banged as he rummaged through it. "One eighth, three quarters, one sixteenth…" He grinned, selecting a piece and screwing it onto the fitting. He dropped the component into the chamber and attached the necessary wires.

The three of them stood silent, staring at the completed engine.

"Go ahead, honey." Justin rested his hand on Alexa's lower back and Jason reached out to squeeze her left hand. "Start it up."

She inhaled and looked at them in turn, then nodded. They held a collective breath as she pushed the ignition button.

The engine roared to life.

For a moment, they stood stunned. Then Alexa squealed and dragged them both to her, kissing Justin as her arm crushed Jason's waist.

She faced Jason. "You gave us the key." She followed her words with a sweet, tender kiss that sucked the breath from his lungs.

He smirked as she turned to Justin. The pride and desire in her eyes melted his brother. Justin swooped back in for another quick kiss before she whispered, "And you made it work."

They both said, "But we couldn't have done it without you."

"Jinx." Her laughter was infectious.

She reached out and shut off the engine. "What do we do now?"

"I set up an appointment with a patent officer for first thing tomorrow morning. I knew you two would figure this out." Jason had used his connections to score a time slot that usually took months to schedule. "There's nothing else we can do until then."

"I can think of a thing or two to pass the time." Justin's wicked smile left no room for misunderstanding. "Let's celebrate."

CHAPTER NINE

"**I**'ve died and gone to heaven," Alexa purred.

She reclined on the huge, downy bed in what she had come to think of as her room. The twins alternated feeding her from a decadent selection of berries, cheese and champagne as they lay propped up on either side of her. Naked, their statuesque bodies made a feast for her eyes that rivaled the gourmet food they proffered.

"That would make Justin an angel, which is clearly not accurate." Jason's dry wit made her laugh and some of the sparkling wine Justin held out to her dribbled down her chin, onto her chest, landing above the lacy edge of her turquoise negligee. Both brothers had insisted she keep her underwear on until she ate, but the deepest hunger she had was for them.

She peeked up at Justin to find his stare glued to the curve of her breasts and the droplets of amber liquid pooling on them. Alexa turned to Jason, manipulating his sense of propriety by arching an eyebrow in false indignation. "You're not going to let it stain my bra, are you?"

Justin growled from her other side as Jason's head dipped down and his tongue flashed out, lapping up the spilled champagne. The flowing touch on her skin coaxed a moan from her.

Each brother took one of her shoulders and raised her up. Justin's hand snaked behind her back and untied the top with one smooth flick of his fingers. They each peeled away a side of the garment. Justin removed it, flinging it over the side of the bed, while Jason continued to lick and suck her flesh. He lifted his head and reached for the bottle of expensive bubbly resting in a bucket of ice.

"It's exquisite mixed with the taste of her." The smoky tone of his voice bolstered her arousal as they settled her against the mountain of pillows until she lay nearly horizontal. He tipped the bottle in miniscule increments. She watched the liquid hang over the spout of the bottle as the meniscus stretched, surface tension and his control keeping her in suspense. Then a rivulet poured out onto her chest and meandered down the center of her body inch by inch.

The cool liquid fizzled on her skin for a moment before Justin murmured a low curse and dove for the trail sliding down her. His sultry breath bathed her as his tongue swept the intoxicating drink from her torso. When nothing remained, Jason renewed the flow from the green glass bottle and Justin continued his deliberate cleansing. The contrasting temperatures drew her nipples tight. Jason tugged on the hardened peaks, sending a ray of sparks straight into her core.

Distracted by Justin's mouth, now sipping a larger splash of champagne from her belly button, Alexa didn't see Jason take a raspberry from the silver dish at her side. She jumped when he pressed the fruit against her stomach then drew a heart on her with the sticky red juice. Justin followed the path of the crude drawing and his mouth curved up in a smile against the sensitive surface of her belly.

"It's true, you know," he murmured against her in between licks and nips. "We love you."

Her eyes met Jason's piercing gaze and, in the profound green pools, she recognized his tacit agreement with Justin's declaration. They echoed the overwhelming sense of belonging and homecoming that permeated every fiber of her being in their company. She knew, without a doubt, these two virile men were destined to be her soulmates and she thanked every power she could imagine that she had been given this opportunity for happiness with them.

This is a chance worth taking.

"I'm ready. It's irrational. I've only just met you, but I know it's true." She buried one hand in Justin's hair, tugging the strands with delicate pressure until he looked at her, and palmed the side of Jason's jaw. "I love you, too. Both of you."

Justin's fingers tightened on her hip as he buried his face against her breasts and held her close. Jason leaned down and took her lips in the most romantic kiss of her life. He caressed her with his mouth, stroked her with his tongue and never once looked away from the moisture filling her eyes with happiness. He rested his forehead on hers and rubbed their noses together before pulling back to let his twin have a turn.

Justin's kiss scalded her with the fury of his passion. His big body overwhelmed her when he pressed close, his cock resting against her hip, throbbing in time to the pounding heartbeat vibrating her breast where their chests melded together. Jason traveled down from her neck, stimulating every part of her that he passed. He bit her shoulder hard enough to sting before drawing away the sensation with a soothing sweep of his lips. When he reached her breast, he moaned—a husky sound of need—and drew the aching peak into his mouth. He swirled his tongue around the nipple, causing her to arch against Justin's body, pinning her in place.

Justin fractured the contact between them, descending to mimic the treatment on her other breast. Her feet propped flat on the comforter as she tried to force herself closer to the source of her pleasure. Hands roamed over her abdomen and thighs, and a single fingertip traced the scalloped edge of her panties.

"Yes, please, touch me." She squeezed her thighs together, trying desperately to cause some friction on her clit through the restless movement of her legs.

Jason lifted his head from worshipping her chest and smiled up at her. He covered her mound with his palm. She rubbed against him, too turned on to be embarrassed by her wanton behavior. His long fingers cupped her, the ends tapping against her ass. She shrieked, the sensations too intense at first, then sank by degrees into the resulting delight.

"Do you want to show Justin our surprise?" His innate control returned, guiding their encounter.

She glanced down to the other man eagerly devouring her breast, driving her insane. It would be nice to turn the tables and see him awed by the power of their connection. Alexa nodded, words beyond her capability at present.

The pads of Jason's fingers worked up her slit, stroking her over her underwear. Slick arousal coated them through the fabric, making them glide across the ridges of her silk encased labia. She groaned, a sound she didn't recognize coming from herself, when his finger slipped around the edge and entered the tiniest bit inside her swollen opening.

"Alright, sweetheart. If you're sure." His reassuring nod bolstered her confidence. "Justin, get rid of her underwear."

He grabbed the side seam and ripped, tearing them from her body. The pressure of the band on her skin just before it snapped made her aware of his strength and determination to have her. Still tormenting her chest with his skilled foreplay, he couldn't see what Jason referred to and didn't seem to be able to tear himself away long enough to find out.

She attempted to hurry them, but they conspired to hold her in place, each pressing against her until, eventually, she gave in and accepted their sweet torture. Jason's finger lodged inside her pussy at the first knuckle. Despite her wetness, even that single digit needed to be cajoled through the muscles clenching furiously around it. He worked her open before adding a second finger.

When the tide of desire overcame her without warning, she naturally looked to Jason for permission. He studied her reactions, observing her with close scrutiny as he manipulated her sensitive pussy. "Wait for it. It'll be better that way."

She grit her teeth, trying to still the rhythmic tightening inside her, but she wouldn't be able to refrain for long.

"Justin, turn her over. Alexa has something she wants to show you." By the way his cock bobbed in excitement, she knew Jason enjoyed it just as much as she did.

The room rotated around her as Justin's strong arms flipped her like she weighed no more than a feather. Her knees curled up instinctively and she rested on all fours, her head and shoulders lying against the pillows, her ass thrust up into the air.

"Oh fuck!" Lust distorted Justin's voice into a rapsy expression of desire. She nearly collapsed when he caressed the base of the anal plug tucked inside her ass. "Were you wearing that the whole time we were downstairs?"

"Yes!" she shouted. Whether in answer to his question, or because the vibration of his exploratory touch felt so damn amazing, she didn't know. Justin swept light kisses across her displayed ass cheeks while Jason thrust his fingers deeper inside her channel.

"Shit, I almost came just thinking about that." Justin's rough laugh accompanied a crisp spank. She jumped in surprise, increasing the contact. His cock rubbed against her leg as his hips rocked and his touch rimmed her rear entrance near the intrusion. "You have no idea how sexy this is. I can see your hole spasm around it when I touch you."

Jason's fingers rotated, stroking the wall of her pussy, trapping it against the pliable object on the other side. "Please, let me come. Someone fuck me, please." She could hear irregular breathing behind her and knew they couldn't tease her much longer.

"Will you let me take your ass, honey?" Justin displayed uncharacteristic self-control as he waited for her answer. His fingertip trembled on her ultra-sensitive ring of muscle.

A grain of trepidation snuck past her guard. Before she could filter it out, she asked, "Will it hurt?"

"Probably," he admitted though it didn't sound as though that would deter him. "At first, almost definitely, but I bet Jason can distract you." He pressed harder now. His finger prodded the opening a bit wider, causing a moan to break free from her chest. The new sensation excited her far more than it scared her.

"Yes." She moaned as his hand disappeared suddenly. "Do it."

The bed dipped as he left and she would have felt abandoned if not for Jason holding her steady. While Justin was gone, Jason raised her leg and slid beneath it so he lay on his back under her and she straddled his face. His breath whispered over her clit and Alexa dropped down, pressing her soaked pussy against his mouth. She rode his lips while he firmed his tongue and began poking it inside her. Every time she thought she would fall over the edge into climax, he nipped the outer edges of her pussy enough to return her control.

She got lost in the seduction of Jason's mouth and was startled when something cool and slippery ran down the crack of her ass. Justin had returned and began preparing her. She shuddered in anticipation, causing her clit to rub across the tip of Jason's tongue. "Hurry. Please."

"That's not the way you want to do this." Justin's voice came close to her ear as he bent over her back. He greased the base of the plug, swiping his fingers in a circle around it, spreading the lubricant over her asshole. "You're going to have to push out now, baby. On three. Ready?"

Jason kept licking her pussy, driving her wild, and Justin stroked her flank with one hand.

"Yes." Alexa prepared herself.

"One." He counted as he took the base in a firm grip with one hand. "Two. Three." She almost forgot to follow his directions because the bulbous middle of the toy stretched her to impossible proportions. It felt so much larger than it had when Jason penetrated her with it earlier. She stiffened, causing the pain to worsen. Justin inserted two fingers inside her pussy and caressed the rough patch of her G-spot, unfreezing her with waves of heat that melted her defiance.

The widest segment of the toy passed her anus and the rest slipped from her with a pop. She moaned and her hole flexed against the cool air. Justin growled behind her and she heard the toy thunk to the ground, forgotten.

"Oh God. You should see this, Jay." But Justin had already positioned himself behind her. He rubbed the full head of his cock against the susceptible opening. "It's nice and stretched open for me."

Alexa noted the snick of a flip cap before he squeezed a generous dollop of lube onto his cock, heard the wet, fleshy sounds it made when he took the engorged length in his fist and slathered the slick substance over it. Then he scooped the excess warmed gel into her waiting orifice. Her body convulsed in response, tightening all her muscles, clenching around Jason's hand. He moaned against her pussy.

"Jay, I want her to come. I want her to enjoy it when I slide my cock inside her sexy ass for the first time." Justin's hands clamped on either side of her waist drawing her to him until the tip of his cock fit against her.

The suspense drove her wild. She lurched back, trying to fill the emptiness with his hard-on but Justin dodged her movement. The crack of his palm on her ass resounded in the room but the resulting burn only heightened her arousal.

Jason sucked her clit into his mouth on a groan when she said, "Again. Please, spank me harder."

A harsh laugh came from behind her. "That's Jason's specialty, honey, but don't try to force this. You're too tight to take all of my cock at once."

Peeking over her shoulder, she saw him wrap his hand around his fully erect cock and guide it to her ass. Jason stopped eating her long enough to watch the action close up as Justin crouched over them both. A constant pressure built against her rear entrance and his mouth flattened in a grimace as he restrained himself from thrusting inside her.

"You have to let me in, baby." With the tip of his cock nudging inside, he leaned forward, blanketing her back so he whispered encouragement directly in her ear. "Relax, trust me."

"I do." She promised, concentrating on loosening the muscles. "I trust you."

His cock penetrated another fraction of an inch, setting off an avalanche of sensation. Pleasure, pain, shock and longing mixed in a whimper that sounded more animal than human.

"That's it, honey." He kissed her cheek, his gentleness at odds with the tension broadcast by his tight abdomen. Jason renewed his efforts, the double stimulation causing her eyes to close as she fought to hold herself together.

"You're doing great, push back against me. The head of my cock is almost inside you now. The rest will be easier."

His constant stream of commentary made it all too easy to visualize what he did to her. It added another layer of ecstasy to the moment. Jason increased the suction on her clit and drove a third finger inside her. The combination of his mouth and hands with Justin's cock and dirty talk were unstoppable. She surrendered to the rush of sensation.

Justin sank several inches deep when the clasp of her ass relaxed in the instant before she shattered. Jason's fingers scissored inside her, spreading her pussy even as it clamped around him. Full to bursting, Justin bore inside her more completely with every surge of his hips. It hurt, more than a little, but pleasure consumed her and drowned out the pain.

"Fuck!" He buried himself further, rasping against pleasure centers she didn't know existed, prolonging her climax. "That's it. Come on my cock, squeeze it so tight."

Jason sucked her clit with steady draws of his hot mouth, swiping the arousal running from her into his mouth periodically, until she couldn't take anymore and tried to squirm away.

"Oh, no you don't. You're not finished." Justin clutched his arm around her middle, pinning her back tight against his front, then turned them both so he reclined on the bed, with his shoulders leaning against the headboard, and she sat on his ripped abdomen. She collapsed against the muscled expanse of his chest, trying to catch her breath as gravity impaled her on the entire length of his shaft.

"You're too big." Her disgruntled complaint met with his strained laughter.

"Seems just right to me." He kissed her neck, fanning the embers of desire until they rekindled to her amazement. She turned her head and greeted his seeking lips in an unspoken, passionate communication. She lay, cushioned by his strength, his stature emphasizing her petite build. Alexa felt loved, secure, treasured, and knew he understood her reciprocal emotions in the same intuitive way.

Jason rolled to his knees and crawled between their legs. His hands encircled her waist as he positioned her to fit better against his twin. He lifted her a few inches, then guided her down until her ass rested snug to Justin's pelvis.

"Son of a bitch, Jay," He snarled, his teeth clenched. "I'm going to come right now if you don't leave her alone. She's so hot, her orgasm's lingering, squeezing her ass around my cock."

He groaned and his head banged against the headboard as he fought for control.

Jason grinned down at her, petting her chest, stroking down to the sensitive spot just above her pussy. Her muscles clamped in response and Justin thrust his hips, grinding into her.

"Can you handle both of us, sweetheart?" Jason's hand sheathed his cock, as he idly stroked up and down the long shank glistening with precome.

"I'm going to try." She reached out, bringing him close for a kiss. She tasted her own sweetness on his mouth and suddenly she needed him as though she hadn't just had the most intense orgasm of her life.

Justin cupped her breasts, weighing them in his palms before tweaking her nipples. She arched into his touch, increasing the pressure. Jason's cock lay at the apex of her thighs, gliding through her slit as he sucked her tongue into his mouth. She tilted her hips and the dark purple head nudged against her wet hole.

"Shit, yes." Justin moaned beneath them, his hands shifting to guide her hips, lifting and dropping her on his engorged flesh. The motion wedged Jason's cock inside her further and stretched her with both of their girths. "I can feel him opening your pussy. Take us. Take us both."

Jason retreated enough to allow them to watch his cock disappearing inside her with rapt attention. As he began to thrust, delving deeper and deeper, she could no longer hold herself up and her head fell back against Justin's collarbone. Just when she thought she couldn't take it anymore, Jason changed the angle of his penetration and slid home.

All three of them lay still for an instant, caught by the raw power flowing between them before Jason and Justin began to fuck her simultaneously. They moved inside her, deep and hard, gaining speed and groaning louder in her ears. Overflowing with their heat and power, she relinquished all control and gave herself over to their demands.

One of Justin's hands moved to her mound, his fingers split in a V around Jason's cock plunging inside her with full, furious strokes. He traced the seam of her pussy up to her clit and began to rub it in small circles she couldn't resist.

"Yes," Jason shouted above her as his pubic bone forced Justin's fingers to tap against her clit. "I can feel you gathering. Let go. Come for us."

Jason slammed inside her, shoving her back against Justin's sheltering embrace even as he drove into her from behind, sandwiching her between them. Their cocks pinched the thin layer of skin separating them, stroking it with provocative glides of their steel-hard flesh.

Alexa came, shuddering in their arms, cresting one peak only to be propelled to another by their shuttling cocks. Behind her, Justin bellowed his release a fraction of a second before Jason ground and bucked against her. Their cocks pulsed together, wringing another climax from her as they spilled their semen inside her. Come filled her pussy and ass as jet after jet spurted onto swollen, sensitive tissue.

Pleasure overwhelmed her and she collapsed, pliant onto Justin's chest. She only became aware of the room around her and the men embedded in her heart when they rolled to one side, still locked together, sheltering her between them.

Jason brushed her hair away from her eyes and tucked it behind her ear.

"I love you." All three of them whispered the declaration at the same time.

"Jinx. Again." She grinned as her eyes fluttered shut, lulled into a deep sleep by the bone-deep satisfaction coursing through her.

CHAPTER TEN

Justin couldn't stop touching her. Long minutes after Alexa had drifted off to sleep, he continued to stroke her hair in complete awe of the emotions she instilled in his heart. He could no longer imagine his life without her. Jason propped himself on his elbow, tracing a path from her shoulder to her hip with a feather light touch.

Justin broke the reverent silence with a whisper. "Jay."

"Yeah." His brother's lazy, satisfied voice drifted to him.

"She was made for us." He pressed a tender kiss to her forehead. Even in sleep, she angled closer, welcoming his caress.

Jason's eyes turned misty and Justin panicked, afraid his brother might lose his unflappable restraint. "Hey, none of that shit, Jay."

Jason buried his face against the curve of Alexa's neck and nuzzled her, breathing deep of her sweet scent to ground himself. "I just never imagined we'd find her. I couldn't let myself hope. Now, she's here. Our perfect woman. Real. I can't bear the thought that we might fuck it up and lose her."

"I know." Justin recalled countless women they'd shared, none lasting more than a night or two. Though they sated the twins' carnal hungers, he'd watched Jason battle despair each time it became clear they couldn't compliment the brothers out of bed. "That's why I think we should ask her to move in with us after the meeting tomorrow. I can't let her go even when there's no more threat."

Jason agreed. "I can't either. I just hope it's not too soon for her. Justin, we have to be patient. Do whatever it takes to prove to her what we know. She's ours."

"And we're hers." The brothers sealed the pact with a knowing gaze before they wrapped around their woman and joined her in sleep.

***

Justin shifted in the uncomfortable office chair and wondered how Jason and Alexa thrived in such stifling environments. Granted, the musty, dim corridors they'd navigated, past dingy, government-issue cubical walls differed vastly from the elegant fixtures of his brother's high-end building, but any office seemed like a cattle pen to him. Trapped here day after day without even a glimpse of the sun he would go insane.

Alexa, on the other hand, had tugged her suit jacket around her slender shoulders like armor earlier this morning and turned with a grin to leave as though she anticipated the task. In fact, when they arrived, she dove into the duty of convincing the squat man with thick glasses of their eligibility to claim the patent for the biofuel engine with a fervor that couldn't be entirely false. *She really enjoys this.*

A combination of irrefutable logic, precise language, precedents set by similar cases and her undeniable charm convinced the patent officer. Within fifteen minutes, he ate out of the palm of her hand. While the official hunched over the documents, signing and sealing where appropriate, Justin wondered if a man existed she couldn't wrap around her little finger.

He caught sight of Jason shaking his head in wonder and winked at him. Justin's palms dampened with nervous sweat. Now that this business concluded, they could move on to the future. What if Alexa rejected their proposal? She was a priceless gift, irreplaceable. The thought of losing her caused a bead of perspiration to form on his brow.

Her enthusiasm rescued him from further worry when she rose and pumped the little man's pudgy hand. Justin mimicked Jason, reaching forward in turn to complete the transaction with a handshake of his own. Victory sparkled in her eyes. Her excitement and pride captivated him. She laid her fine-boned fingers on his forearm and subtly guided him from the room while Jason followed close behind.

She waited until the metal doors of the elevator trundled closed, locking the three of them inside, before doing an adorable happy dance that jiggled all the right parts of her anatomy. She smacked a quick kiss on his cheek and squeezed Jason before composing herself in time to maintain her respectable appearance when the lobby opened up in front of them moments later.

"We did it." She passed the briefcase containing copies of the patent documentation to Jason then reached out to hold one of their hands in each of her own as they crossed the polished granite floor. They headed toward the secure garage where they'd arranged to park this morning to avoid the main lot and entryway.

"Wait." Justin stopped short, causing a chain reaction, tugging them all to a halt in the middle of the bustling crowd.

"What's wrong?" Alarm tinged Alexa's reply.

"Nothing." Justin attributed his uneasiness to the life change he and Jason planned to discuss with her when they returned home. Though certain of his desires, he feared scaring her off. Spontaneously, he decided she deserved the proper atmosphere when they asked her to become a permanent part of their lives, something fancier than the living room couch. Jason's connections ensured a table at an exclusive restaurant for lunch. "Let's go out. Le Chic is just around the corner. We should go someplace special." His brother understood what he intended but he shook his head in opposition.

"I don't think that's wise." Jason waggled the handle of the briefcase. "Until this is announced, some risk exists."

Still riding the high of accomplishing their objective, Alexa beamed up at Jason and broke the tie. "It'd be nice to get away for a little bit before all the real work preparing and marketing the product begins. Plus, I've always wanted to eat at Le Chic."

Justin knew his brother couldn't deny her. Jason's trepidation gave way to a shrug and a grin. She had a way of relaxing him. "What the hell? It's just an hour. Sure, let's go."

Together, they pivoted toward the main entrance. Always the gentleman, Jason held the heavy glass and metal door for Alexa who started down the wide limestone staircase with Justin trailing a few feet after her.

Too late, Justin spotted the brawny mercenary who stepped from behind one of the massive fluted pillars, gun drawn, aimed pointblank at Alexa's chest. His leathery face hosted evil eyes, on fire and out of control. Justin could see the man riding the edge of sanity. He'd always pictured assassins as calculating and cold, but this man's emotions flew all over the charts. Now his life, and the lives of the two people who made up his world, were at the mercy of a deranged killer for hire.

"I knew you'd show up here eventually." The grin he flashed revealed crooked, yellow teeth. "Now, toss me the case." The steel conviction brooked no argument but Alexa defied the bastard, sending shards of razor sharp terror through Justin's heart.

"You're too late." She stood firm, blocking the path to Jason. Justin had no opportunity to quiet her or get between her and the deadly threat. "We already patented the design on behalf of Winston Industries and the surviving members of the original research team."

"Liar!" the man snarled. His gun wavered when frustration and rage deteriorated his shaky control. "If I fail to recover the design they'll kill me too."

Justin coiled, preparing to spring at the slightest chance to intercede but no opening presented itself. Jason dismayed him further by edging to the side, drawing the insane light burning in the gunman's eyes onto himself.

"Here. Take it." He thrust the leather satchel outward. "Just let her go."

"The bitch is right, it's worthless! Unless the patent holders are dead." The man's trigger finger tightened, his knuckles white on the grip of the pistol.

Jason flung the case at the man's arm at the same instant Justin launched for Alexa. He tackled her, tucking around her in mid-air, attempting to shield her. The rapid double bang of the gun firing twice, before the case knocked it from the man's hold, corresponded to the sick lurch of her body now falling beneath him, making it obvious he had failed.

Jason's primordial scream of fury and pain echoed the despair flashing into Justin's soul. Some far corner of his brain registered the dull thud of fist on face accompanying Jason's dispatch of the monster who had tried to destroy their future. Justin left their defense to Jason and concentrated on their woman.

"Alexa!" he cried as the first hot gush of her blood streamed through his fingers clenching her back. Terrified to see the extent of the damage, he pulled himself away from her limp body. A giant crimson stain spread across the right side of her upper chest. Simultaneously horrified and relieved, he watched the blood throb from the gaping hole in her tattered shirt in time to her racing heartbeat. At least she still had a heartbeat.

Jason fell down beside them and applied pressure to staunch the wound with the jacket he yanked from his shoulders. A painful, unnatural sound emanated from the mask of shock her face had become as she gasped for air. She attempted to get up but her blood-slicked hand slipped feebly on the stone beneath her.

"Oh God, no." Justin stared at her in abject horror.

Jason worked over her with deliberate efficiency but Justin could only gape.

"Lie still, sweetheart." His brother's calm reassurance worked on Justin as well. He gripped Alexa's hand, trying to conjure a million words at once. He needed to tell her so many things. He couldn't bear for her to die never knowing she was their life.

"Jason. Justin." Their names rasped wetly between her shallow wheezing. Blood flecked her luscious lips when she whispered. "Love you."

Justin's chance to pledge it in return disappeared when her eyelids closed, every muscle in her body lax, and his sanity evaporated.

CHAPTER ELEVEN

Jason tamped down the cocktail of frustration, pain and concern brewing within him as he stared at his brother, feeling more helpless than ever before in his life. Justin drooped, half reclined in the hospital bed. IVs hydrated him to assist his recovery from the loss of blood he'd suffered but Jason figured his blanched complexion had more to do with their argument than the bullet wound piercing the thick muscle of his twin's upper arm.

His dumbass brother hadn't even realized he'd been shot. Overcome by dread and misery he'd plowed on to the hospital, only receiving treatment when he collapsed in the waiting room. Thankfully, the doctor assured them the damage would heal with minimal inconvenience.

The same did not hold true for Alexa.

Bile rose in his throat for the millionth time since he'd watched the sinister handgun come up in front of her. No matter how often he replayed the scene in his mind, analyzing the options, no other possible outcome presented itself. They'd done all they could.

"I'll never forgive myself for what happened today." Justin's misery permeated every word, every movement, every breath he took.

"Damn it." Jason couldn't bear to lose his brother on top of everything else that'd transpired today. He continued attempting to convince him. With a firm hand on his shoulder, he subdued his weakened twin. "You're being ridiculous. Don't go. This is not your fault."

"You warned me of the danger. I ignored you. I risked her life but she suffered the consequences." Justin didn't seem aware of the tears making silent tracks down his face. Panic flared in Jason's chest, he hadn't seen his brother cry since childhood. "Fuck! Why can't I ever fucking think about these things before I do something so fucking stupid?"

"We made a mistake, Justin. I agreed, too. Slow down. Consider the consequences this time."

Despair clouded Justin's rationality. "No, I don't deserve to be around you. I'll only fuck up your life more than I already have."

"We're two halves of the same whole, remember?" Stark terror had chilled Jason earlier, when he feared he might lose both Alexa and Justin. It had reinforced the importance of their bond. "I need you now more than ever."

"Me. Too." The faint, scratchy words barely rose above the whir and beep of all the hospital equipment but Jason and Justin both whipped around to see Alexa fighting to stay awake.

"Sweetheart." Jason hovered over her, his chest constricting when he witnessed her labored breathing. "Thank God."

Behind them, he heard muffled curses and the rip of tape as Justin tore the tubes and needles from his arm before stumbling to her bedside. Jason grabbed a chair and pushed his brother down into it with one hand, the other never leaving her tentative grip as she tried to catch her breath after her brief speech.

***

The slow, fractured words scraped Alexa's throat, causing her to wince. A dull ache infused every cell of her body. Disoriented, the now familiar cadence of her lovers arguing drew her from a fog of suffering. A sense of urgency propelled her to full consciousness.

The strained lines of worry creasing Jason's handsome face frightened her as much as the liquid agony dripping from the less reserved brother's eyes.

"I nearly got you killed." Self-loathing oozed from Justin.

She grappled with the situation, trying to force it to make sense, all the while resisting the insistent lull of her drug induced weariness. She blinked in an attempt to bring the room around her into sharper focus. Breathing hurt beyond belief, her throat dried from the oxygen pumping into her, and she couldn't force her vocal cords to produce the questions she needed to ask.

"Just rest. Don't struggle." Jason bent low over her to brush his lips across her forehead. "I love you more than you'll ever know. The doctor says you're going to be okay. I'll be right here with you, and so will Justin. You're safe now. Sleep, baby."

She trained her gaze on Justin but he refused to look her in the eye. *Are they lying? Am I going to die?*

"Justin, you're scaring her. Quit being a fool."

"Shit. I'm making things worse, even now. I'll go." He pried himself up to a half crouch before Alexa forced her body to respond to a fraction of her commands. Her hand rose a mere inch off the hospital bed before it dropped, listless at her side.

"No." The grotesque whisper sounded nothing like the shout she intended.

"Honey, don't." Justin laid his head gingerly on the pillow next to her, eyes squeezed shut. "I can't stand to see you hurt."

His bloodshot eyes opened, so close to her own they filled her world. "I love you with all my soul. I'm leaving you with Jay. He's good for you. He'll always take care of you. Protect you."

His abandonment broke something precious inside her. She recalled his hollered promise to love her just a few short days ago. He'd convinced her that he meant it. How could she have been fooled again?

"Liar." The rending of her spirit far surpassed the agony of her body. Comprehension dawned in the depths of his emerald eyes a moment later and she knew he remembered his vow, too.

Jason interceded. "Fine. I never imagined you were such a coward. Leave if you need to run, but quit hurting her. I won't stand for anyone causing her a moment's grief ever again. Get out."

Regret, agony, fear and resignation cycled through Justin's expression. She tried to beg him to stay, to hell with pride, but the darkness crept over her, dragging her down into the medicated void once more.

***

Days passed in a blur of sounds and dreams. Alexa remembered Jason's somber explanation of the surgery necessary to repair her punctured lung. Then sedation prohibited her from discovering anything further.

The next time she surfaced, she woke to darkness. A strong hand entwined with hers prevented her from panicking. She rubbed the pad of her thumb across the warm palm. The lack of calluses convinced her it belonged to Jason. The sweet visions of Justin must have been delusions.

Her light touch roused him from his fitful doze in the chair beside the bulky hospital bed. His arm distended at an awkward angle that had to be uncomfortable.

"You're awake." His sexy, sleep roughened voice allowed her to fantasize she'd stirred in the night to make love to him.

I guess I'm getting better. The sarcastic thought factored in a healthy dose of relief. Her hand clasped Jason's tighter, responding like normal as some of her strength returned. Bolstered by the small success, she tested her voice with the most important message first.

"Love you." The audible phrase sounded clearer than her previous attempt. Joy rushed through her. He had proved the strength of his character by sticking with her. Reliable, gentle, loving and kind, he fulfilled her needs. Well, at least those she allowed herself to acknowledge.

Spontaneity, laughter, adventure, unbridled emotion…What about those? She couldn't return to the half existence she lived before Justin unlocked her wild side and gave her permission to indulge it.

"I love you too, Alexa." The words carried a sacred promise they both understood. They would never be parted or give up on each other.

Tears scalded her dry eyes causing Jason to sit up in alarm. "Are you okay? Should I get the nurse?"

She shook her head, gesturing for him to sit.

"We can't live without…him." She couldn't bring herself to utter Justin's name. An abyss festered deep in her chest where his love should reside.

"Jesus Christ!" Jason's sharp response rose in volume. "How much do you remember?"

"Justin. Left. Us." Her stamina began to fade again, her eyes shutting under the weight of despair.

"Stay awake, baby." He patted her hand, bringing her back a bit. "Just a minute more this time, please? Focus on what I'm saying."

While he talked, he stretched to the table beside her and grabbed the box of tissues. She expected him to dry her tears, not to hurl the carton at the bed on her other side.

A startled grunt filtered from the darkness.

"What the hell was that for, Jay? You hit my fucking arm."

Justin's grumpy mumble sent her pulse flying. The machine beside her clamored with the sudden rise.

"For frightening Alexa," Jason answered. "Now get your ass over here."

Justin asked, concerned, "What's that beeping? I don't recognize that one. Is something wrong?"

His head snapped toward her when he belatedly realized she was conscious. Jason stroked her arm, calming the painful trembling spreading throughout her body.

"You're here." The desperation spilling into her voice would have annoyed her at any other time but, for now, her gratitude crowded out all other thoughts. The lethargy haunting her lifted as euphoria pumped her up.

"I promised." Justin sank down next to her, careful not to jostle the mattress. "I could never leave you. God, have you spent all this time thinking I abandoned you?"

"How long?" It seemed like forever and, yet, just a moment ago that she woke up in this room.

"It's been three weeks of pure hell for us all. Did you really believe I left?" Shame colored his question when he read the truth in her expression. He took her free hand in his, completing the chain with Jason on her other side. He swallowed hard. "I love you, Alexa. The day we got shot, I went a little crazy. Maybe it was the blood loss." His self-deprecating laugh fell flat.

"You? Shot?" She examined him but everything she saw looked like healthy, strapping man.

"Yeah, you guys left me out of the fun. I guess I'm just not cool enough to take a bullet." Jason's humor didn't fully mask his concern. "When Justin dove in front of you, the second shot got him in the arm. If he hadn't knocked you over... Well, it wouldn't have been good. It doesn't seem like it now, baby, but you got so damn lucky. The doctors didn't think you had a chance at first."

"Stubborn." She smiled for the first time since Justin's emotions had made her believe there could be no happy ending for them.

"Thank God," the twins answered together.

"Jinx."

They laughed for her, since the gesture was too painful to attempt, even as contentment settled over her for the first time in weeks. But, still, she had to know if the sensation came from false security.

"Did they catch him?" She hated the fear that seeped into the question.

"Jay took him down." Justin beamed at his twin. "They've got him on multiple counts, including the murder of the informant since they matched the bullet to his gun. Jay called in some of his fancy hotshot lawyers and they swear he's going to bring in the whole operation. He's given them names, locations, descriptions and all the info they need. Besides, the patents have been verified, publically announced, and upheld by the court."

"Thank God." She surrendered to relief, sinking back into the hospital bed as the last of her tension drained out. Drowsiness returned, enhanced by the glow of safety and the comfort of her men holding her hands, stroking her hair and just being near.

"One last thing, sweetheart." Jason's tone turned serious. The nearly palpable loyalty in his eyes made her heart soar. "Recovering is going to take time and determination but we'll be here to support you every step of the way. While you're working on getting better, will you think about moving in with us for good? We want to spend our lives with you if you'll have us."

"Yes." She squeezed their hands and love poured into her from both sides. Justin's gaze burned with desire, commitment and a shred of fear that pushed her to answer. There was no need to leave them in suspense. "No thinking. Just yes."

Jason's intense sincerity balanced Justin's smoldering grin of delight.

"Well, honey." Justin winked at her. "I guess you better concentrate on healing up quicker. Looks like we have a lot more to celebrate now."

They both leaned in and kissed her cheeks before whispering promises of eternal devotion. Alexa drifted into a restful sleep with a smile on her face and love in her soul. The assurance of years of bliss to come fabricated nice and naughty dreams for her to savor.

to the lust that's been arcing between them since day one. In the aftermath of the best sex of her life, she whispers her most secret desire: to be ravaged by his crew.

She never expected Mike would dare her to take what she wants—or that the freedom to make her most decadent desires come true could be the foundation for something lasting...

Warning: This book may cause you to spontaneously combust as five hot guys bring a woman's wildest fantasies to life during one blazing summer affair.

EXCERPT FROM KATE'S CREW, POWERTOOLS BOOK 1

Kate wiped her palms on her paint-splattered cutoffs before adjusting her grip on the rebuilt window casement. A flash of tan skin drew her attention to glistening muscles. They rippled over five sexy frames as the crew renovating the townhouse next door hammered nail after nail into their first-story roof, just a few feet below her perch.

From inside the bedroom where she worked, she inched to the edge of the ladder rung then craned her neck through the opening in front of her for a glimpse of the intricate tattoo spanning Mike's broad shoulders. Instead, she caught him reaching up to their stash of supplies for another pack of shingles. When her gaze latched onto the drop of sweat that slid along his neck, she forgot to breathe. She watched in fascination as it journeyed over his defined pecs and six-pack abs. After it was absorbed in the ultra-low-riding jeans snugged to his trim hips by a bulging tool belt, she heaved a sigh of relief.

Kate swiped at a blob of paint that had plopped onto her wrist unnoticed while she'd ogled Mike. Her tongue moistened her lips as she imagined licking a similar trail down his body. The edge of the fresh trim gouged her thigh as she strained for a better view. The gasp she made busted her. His head lifted, catching her spying. Great, now she'd never convince him to take it easy with his persistent innuendo or date invites. And, no matter how much she wanted to, she couldn't indulge either of their desires.

Mike threw her a dazzling victory grin. The anticipation sparkling in his cocky stare blasted a shockwave through her, screwing with her balance. The ladder wobbled then tipped. She probably could have righted herself if she hadn't been standing on tiptoes to maximize her view of the scenery. In slow motion, she watched his expression morph from flirtatious to horrified.

Kate flung out her arms in an attempt to catch the frame before she tumbled through it but the momentum swung her around. Her temple grazed the custom-made pewter latch she'd installed the day before. She hung, suspended in midair, as Mike rose from his crouch. The other guys began to turn toward her, but he was already sprinting for the edge.

Terror froze her insides when he launched himself across the ten-foot gap between their houses. Then she spun away, losing sight of him. She braced for imminent impact.

Shit, this is going to hurt.

Everything happened at once. Air whooshed from her lungs when she slammed, on her side, onto the roof. She rolled, flexing her ankles in an attempt to find purchase that would halt her skid toward the brink. But her knee wrenched at an awkward angle while she continued to rake over the slate. Her hand caught the ridge of an attic vent, slowing her descent, but gravity overcame the tenuous hold. Her frantic fingers recoiled from the sharp metal edge.

The gutters rushed closer, her last hope. After that, she'd have to pray the evergreen shrubs would cushion her, preventing any broken bones. The heels of her work boots hit the aluminum edging but kept going. Her legs dangled in thin air.

Then a strong hand banded around her wrist. Her arm nearly jerked from the socket as she lurched to a stop. Kate shoved on the edging shingles with her free hand, fighting to stay on the roof.

"Son of a bitch!" Mike hauled her the rest of the way up.

ABOUT THE AUTHOR

Jayne Rylon is a *New York Times* and *USA Today* bestselling author. She received the 2011 RomanticTimes Reviewers' Choice Award for Best Indie Erotic Romance.

Her stories used to begin as daydreams in seemingly endless business meetings, but now she is a full-time author, who employs the skills she learned from her straight-laced corporate existence in the business of writing. She lives in Ohio with two cats and her husband, the infamous Mr. Rylon.

When she can escape her purple office, Jayne loves to travel the world, SCUBA dive, take pictures, avoid speeding tickets in her beloved Sky and—of course—read.

www.ingramcontent.com/pod-product-compliance
Lightning Source LLC
Chambersburg PA
CBHW060752210726
48292CB00014B/2766